DEC 1 7 2015

W9-DAJ-476

Song of Praise

Praise Him Anyhow Series

Song of Praise

Vanessa
Miller

Book 9
Praise Him Anyhow Series

WILLARD LIBRARY, BATTLE CREEK, MI

Publisher's Note:
This short story is a work of fiction. References to real events, organizations, or places are used in a fictional context. Any resemblances to actual persons, living or dead are entirely coincidental.

Vanessa Miller
www.vanessamiller.com

Printed in the United States of America
© 2013 by Vanessa Miller

Praise Unlimited Enterprises
Charlotte, NC

No part of this ebook may be reproduced or transmitted in any form or by any means, electronic or mechanical—including photocopying, recording, or by any information storage and retrieval system—without permission in writing from the publisher.

Other Books by Vanessa Miller

After the Rain
How Sweet The Sound
Heirs of Rebellion
Feels Like Heaven
Heaven on Earth
The Best of All
Better for Us
Her Good Thing
Long Time Coming
A Promise of Forever Love
A Love for Tomorrow
Yesterday's Promise
Forgotten
Forgiven
Forsaken
Rain for Christmas (Novella)
Through the Storm
Rain Storm
Latter Rain
Abundant Rain
Former Rain

Anthologies (Editor)
Keeping the Faith
Have A Little Faith
This Far by Faith

EBOOKS

Love Isn't Enough

A Mighty Love

The Blessed One (Blessed and Highly Favored series)

The Wild One (Blessed and Highly Favored Series)

The Preacher's Choice (Blessed and Highly Favored Series)

The Politician's Wife (Blessed and Highly Favored Series)

The Playboy's Redemption (Blessed and Highly Favored Series)

Tears Fall at Night (Praise Him Anyhow Series)

Joy Comes in the Morning (Praise Him Anyhow Series)

A Forever Kind of Love (Praise Him Anyhow Series)

Ramsey's Praise (Praise Him Anyhow Series)

Escape to Love (Praise Him Anyhow Series)

Praise For Christmas (Praise Him Anyhow Series)

His Love Walk (Praise Him Anyhow Series)

Could This Be Love (Praise Him Anyhow Series)

Song of Praise (Praise Him Anyhow Series)

Song of Praise

Vanessa
Miller

Book 9
Praise Him Anyhow Series

Prologue

Looking out of the window from the twenty-first floor of his hotel room, RaShawn Thomas watched the people go about their business. Carrying packages, coming in and out of restaurants, smiling and laughing as they walked the streets. The people didn't seem the least bit aware of the destruction that was to come. But as sure as the flood waters of hurricane Katrina devastated New Orleans, and as sure as a tsunami could ravage and cripple a nation before they even knew what hit them, so too would be the way of the destruction that was to come. All that was required to turn back God's planned destruction was for the people to repent, but sadly, this nation and others like it was taking pleasure in their sins. They thought they had won, and that the truth of God had lost. Not realizing that God doesn't bow to any man or any sin, no matter how the world tries to dress it up.

Last night as he opened his Bible and turned to Jeremiah 51:20, RaShawn felt as if the Lord was speaking directly to him as he read:

Thou art my battle axe and weapons of war: for with thee will I break in pieces the nations, and with thee will I destroy kingdoms.

RaShawn had no understanding as to how he would break nations or destroy kingdoms, but he knew for sure that the Lord had ordered his steps all the way to Washington, DC. When his sister, Raven had called and asked him to come to Richmond, Virginia to be a spiritual advisor for her husband, Marcus Allen, he'd wondered then what God was up to. His brother-in-law had won the election and as governor of Virginia, Marcus and Raven were doing the Lord's work and doing right by the people in their state.

When RaShawn received the call concerning his new assignment, he felt as if God had released him from watching his brother-in-law's back. God had Marcus, and now the Lord was sending him on a new mission.

RaShawn had started his ministry service on the mission field. While doing the Lord's work in one country after the next, he had encountered demonic forces that tried to stop his mission. But God had always made a way of escape for RaShawn. As he left the hotel and walked down the street towards his new assignment, a chill went through RaShawn's body as he felt the presence of demonic forces that were much stronger than any he had ever encountered.

Looking up to heaven, RaShawn silently prayed, *Lord, be my strength.*

As he entered the church, RaShawn clearly heard the Lord respond.

I will, now go forth and be my battle axe.

The senior bishop of the fellowship met him in the entryway, shook his hand and said, "You made it safely, good. Come on in."

"Before we get started," RaShawn began as they walked down the hall towards his new office, "I'd just like to thank you for selecting me for this position."

Senior Bishop David Brown opened the door to the office and said, "I don't think you'll be thanking me once you see the mess you've inherited."

Chapter One

Be not conformed to this world: but be ye transformed by the renewing of your mind, that ye may prove what is that good and acceptable and perfect will of God.

(Romans 12:2)

Murder isn't so hard, the killer thought, looked at the lifeless body of the victim the killer felt no remorse. How could one feel remorse when murder hadn't actually been committed—this was an assisted suicide. The man's sins had killed him. Now the Avenger of Sins, AKA the killer, sat down at the sinful man's desk and turned on the computer. The Avenger of Sins opened the man's email box and wrote a quick note, addressing it to Bishop RaShawn Thomas and put the killers real name on the signature line. The Avenger gasped as the name appeared on the computer screen, but then hit the backspace key several times.

Done with the email the Avenger clicked the Send button. The Avenger then walked back over to the dead man to spit on the body. But then thought about DNA, and what a shame it would be if the Avengers deeds were discovered because of something done on impulse. If that happened the Avenger wouldn't be able to finish the mission. And if the mission failed, then the Avenger wouldn't be able to exist—for after all, the Avenger was born to set the captives free. Instead of spitting on the dead man, the Avenger of Sins lifted a foot and kicked him in the ribs. The killer wanted to stomp him, but the Avenger remembered a show on Court TV where a killer was discovered because his shoe print was at the crime scene. The Avenger loved Reality TV; they always provided such good information.

The Avenger put the calling card on top of the body. Walking out of the room, the Avenger smiled as the thought of how much better the world would be with one more dead preacher.

***

"No. No, this is not happening. Not again," Bishop RaShawn Thomas said as he read his email. Some maniac was killing off the preachers within his fellowship and sending him emails about the awful deed. RaShawn had called the police immediately after receiving the last two emails, but it hadn't done him any good. By the time the police arrived at the homes of Pastor William Johnson and Pastor Nicolas Brown they were already dead. So RaShawn wasn't waiting this time. He would call the police on his way to Pastor Tony Hartman's home.

RaShawn grabbed his keys and then jumped into his Range Rover, all the while praying that he wasn't too late.

Tony Hartman had given him more trouble than any of the preachers within his fellowship. The man was arrogant, self-serving and a womanizer; all of which served as the reasons RaShawn had asked the man to step down from his position. Since he'd taken over as bishop he'd asked a total of six pastors to step down.

RaShawn was a man with a true heart for God and therefore, he wanted to work with pastors who had the same hunger and passion that he had. The thought of a preacher misusing the children of God turned his stomach. He'd sat silently by and watched these so-called men of God work their way through ministries all his life. They destroyed lives and turned saints away from God with their lust for immorality and greedy ambitions. RaShawn had promised God that if he ever led a fellowship, he would get rid of every pimping preacher and womanizing minister that crossed his path. However, RaShawn never imagined that his goal of clearing out immorality amongst the leadership would result in murder.

Speeding down Interstate 285 headed to Tony's house, RaShawn pulled out his cell phone. He dialed Detective Jarod Harris' cell number. Detective Harris had been assigned to Pastor William Johnson's case and then subsequently assigned to Pastor Nicolas Brown's case. After Brown's murder, Detective Harris had handed RaShawn his business card and said, "If you run into any more dead preachers, call my cell phone."

RaShawn had hoped the detective's comment was nothing more than a bad joke and that he would never need to talk to Jarod Harris again in life, but here he was, waiting for the detective to answer the phone.

"Detective Harris."

RaShawn heard the greeting and almost hung up. He had never been through anything like this in all his life. He had grown up in ministry, and in all his thirty-two years, had never heard of a preacher being murdered in his own home.

"This is Detective Harris; is anyone there?"

"Oh, yes, Detective. This is Bishop RaShawn Thomas."

"Don't tell me that another one of your preachers has gotten himself killed."

Not wanting to accept that Pastor Tony was actually dead, RaShawn only confirmed, "I just received another email."

"Who is it this time?" Jarod asked, sounding a little irritated.

"The email was about Pastor Tony Hartman."

"Tony Hartman! I watch his program, *This is Your Moment* all the time," Jarod said, sounding a little more interested now.

"Can you meet me at his house?"

"Yeah. What's his address?"

RaShawn gave the detective the address and then hung up the phone. He was saddened by the shock in Detective Harris' tone, but a lot of people would be shocked to know that the same preacher who taught millions how to claim their moment and how to always be in the midst of God's perfect timing was the same man who regularly solicited prostitutes and had been carrying on a three-year affair with a stripper named Peaches.

RaShawn prayed that Tony was still alive as he pulled up behind the man's Bentley, jumped out of his SUV and began pounding on the front door. "Tony, are you in there?"

He knocked on the door several more times, calling Tony's name without receiving a response. Tony's wife, Carla had divorced him a year ago, so RaShawn didn't expect that she would open the door or be in the house to help Tony in his time of need. He grabbed the door knob and turned it. The door opened. But instead of RaShawn rejoicing, he inwardly cringed because he knew that Tony never left his door unlocked. Checking each room one by one, RaShawn kept calling Tony's name.

When he reached Tony's home office towards the back of the house on the first floor, RaShawn found Tony stretched out on the floor. He ran to the preacher and knelt down beside him. He lifted his wrist to feel for a pulse. RaShawn then noticed two things at once: There was no pulse and there was a note card lying on Tony's chest. The card had a message. It read, *You do right, and I won't do wrong.*

"Bishop Thomas, are you in here?"

RaShawn heard Detective Harris as he entered the house. He wanted to go greet the man but he didn't want to leave Tony. That fact was ironic to him now, since a couple of weeks ago he wanted to not just get far away from Tony, but to strip the man of his license to preach the gospel. "I'm in here," he hollered.

"Is he dead?" Detective Harris asked as he entered the room.

RaShawn nodded.

"Does he have a card on his chest?"

RaShawn nodded again.

"Did you touch it?"

"No. It was right side up on his chest. I was able to read what it says without touching it." RaShawn turned to Detective Harris with a stunned expression on his face. "Was this note on the other bodies as well?"

"Yes, but we haven't released that information to the public." Detective Harris stepped toward the body as he said, "You shouldn't be in here."

"I had hoped to find him alive." RaShawn rubbed his forehead with the palm of his hand as he stood up. "I honestly don't know how much more of this I can take. I don't understand why this maniac has decided to kill the pastors I fired."

"You fired Pastor Hartman! The man was an icon. I didn't think anyone but God had the authority to fire a man like him."

RaShawn lowered his head as his shoulders slumped.

Putting a hand on the bishop's shoulder, Jarod said, "You can't blame yourself, Bishop. Whoever killed these men did exactly what he wanted to do."

There was no blood. But RaShawn hadn't expected to see any. Detective Harris hadn't communicated much about the other two men's deaths, but he had informed RaShawn that the preachers had been poisoned. RaShawn looked around the room, trying to discover what someone could have used to poison Tony. His eyes drifted to a bottle of grape juice, crumpled crackers and a single wine glass on the desk in Tony's home office. "The poison is in the grape juice, isn't it?"

"In the last two cases the poison had only been in the glass, but not in the bottle of grape juice," Detective Harris said, and then quickly added, "That does not leave this room. We haven't released that information to the public either."

RaShawn turned back toward Tony Hartman and rubbed his forehead with his palm again.

"I'm going to call this in," Detective Harris said. "I need you to wait in the living room so I can question you once I get things in order. And try not to beat me to the next crime scene. Okay?"

Bishop RaShawn wearily walked out of the room and sat down in the living room as he was instructed. He didn't plan to beat Detective Harris to the next crime scene, because RaShawn hoped and prayed that there wouldn't be another one. He had every intention of begging and pleading for police protection for the last three preachers that he recently fired.

He waited while Detective Harris ushered other police officers and forensic technicians into the crime scene. He was sure that Detective Harris would want to speak with him once they had taken care of Tony, so he just kept waiting. RaShawn wished he had remembered to bring the email that he'd received, but the last two emails hadn't provided much of anything to go on. The person sending the messages used a different computer and location with each message.

RaShawn watched as one of the detectives carried the grape juice and wine glass out in a Ziplock bag. It was somehow out of place to see just one wine glass with grape juice. After all, it wasn't actual wine that Tony had been drinking, which he was sure the man indulged in privately. But why would he drink grape juice in a wine glass by himself? RaShawn associated grape juice with communion. Would Tony have taken communion by himself or did the killer also drink it? That would explain why the bottle wasn't tainted. The killer must have poured the poison in Tony's glass and then had communion with him. *But why communion?* RaShawn wondered.

The Bible clearly states in I Corinthians 11:27, "Whosoever shall eat this bread, and drink this cup of the Lord, unworthily, shall be guilty of the body and blood of the Lord." Is that what the mad man was trying to tell them?

RaShawn had no problem understanding the note that was left on Tony's body, but this communion thing was a mystery to him. A murderer and a whoremonger had no reason to partake in communion, did they?

"There's a camera crew outside. You might want to give his next of kin a quick call before they hear about this on the news," Detective Harris told RaShawn as he walked into the living room.

"Me? But I fired the man. His sister was smoking mad at me for that; no way does she want to hear from me right now."

"I can do it myself, but it's going to be a while. I just thought you might want to beat the afternoon news." Detective Harris nodded toward the big picture window in the living room.

RaShawn looked outside and saw just what the detective had been referring to. Camera crews from several news stations were lining the street just below Tony's driveway. He turned back around and said, "I'll call her."

RaShawn took out his cell phone, dreading the call he had to make to Judge Lisa Hartman. But as he began punching in the number, RaShawn changed his mind about which Hartman he would call. Tony's niece, Britney and

RaShawn had history. Two years ago, he and his sister, Raven had saved Britney from a crazy lady who'd wanted to kill her because she'd made the mistake of not only sleeping with the woman's husband, but getting pregnant by him. The ordeal had caused Britney to miscarry.

After the miscarriage, Britney decided to no longer wallow in the pain of her past and got busy cleaning up her act. She was now working as an insurance fraud investigator. She and her mother still weren't on the best of terms, due to her past behavior, but maybe something like this could help to bring mother and daughter back together.

Even knowing that he should call Judge Hartman, it mattered more to RaShawn to find out how this whole thing would affect Britney. He dialed her number and waited for her to pick up. When she did, there was laughter in her voice and RaShawn hated that he was about to take the joy she had found away from her.

Chapter Two

Running late as usual, Britney Hartman threw her camera around her neck as she grabbed a bag of chips, a banana, blueberry muffin and a Mountain Dew—stake out food. She was hot on the trail of a man she believed to be defrauding his employer with a false workman's compensation claim. The guy had worked as a roofer and claimed that he hurt his back and neck falling from a two-story home. Britney had been following him for two weeks now; so far he had been careful. Always making sure to wear his neck brace and carrying his cane around like he was a ninety-year-old man. But yesterday, Britney noticed that Jason Malvern, the man who was on workman's comp, was having work done on his roof. When she arrived at his home, Britney had been thrilled at what she saw. He hadn't actually climbed the ladder or taken a hammer to any of the roofing material; that would have been the money shot. But he hadn't been wearing his neck brace, and his cane had magically disappeared also.

Britney was hopeful that Jason would get on that roof today as she sat in her car watching him chug down a beer with the roofer guy. She was parked one block over, in the perfect spot to see everything that was going on in the back of Jason's house. The only problem was, Britney had noticed a ladder propped against the front of the house and one propped against the back of the house. Yesterday there had only been the one ladder in the back. So, now Britney was eating her chips and praying that Jason would get on the ladder in the back and not the one in the front of the house. Because if he got on the one in the front, she would be forced to either run around front to snap his picture or drive around there. Either way, Jason might spot her and she didn't want that.

Britney had been an investigator for a year and a half now. There was never a boring day in her career. Working for an insurance company, she had been assigned to investigate everything from wrongful death cases to stolen jewelry. Britney always followed her instincts and let her employer know up front whether she thought she was on the trail of a fraud or not. If all those years of drug abuse had taught her nothing else, it had taught her how to spot a fraud—because she had been one.

Her phone rang. Britney looked at the caller ID and saw that it was her best friend, Rita Knox. She normally didn't answer calls when she was on a stake out, but Rita was one of the rare exceptions to that rule. At one time, she and Rita had been pregnant by the same man. The man, a United States senator, had been killed by his wife. Rita had delivered her baby three months after his death. However, Britney had miscarried. Even though the two women could have gone their separate ways after Bishop RaShawn had saved them from that terrible ordeal, she and Rita had become friends and Britney helped her friend with babysitting services… even while she prayed that she would one day have the opportunity to marry the man of her dreams and give birth to his children.

"What's up," Britney said as she answered the phone, careful to keep her eyes on her subject.

"What are you doing?"

"I'm on an assignment. Is everything okay with Tyler?" Rita had named her daughter Tyler. Britney thought it was the perfect name.

"She's taking a nap."

"Did you need anything, or can I call you back when I'm done?"

"No. I need to talk to you now," Rita snapped.

Rita's voice was full of fear.

"Why do you sound like that? What's wrong?"

"Something bad is going to happen. I can feel it."

Ever since the senator's wife had held them hostage and threatened to kill them for having affairs with her husband, Rita had been on edge and nervous about everything. The woman hadn't been able to move on with her life, which was why Britney helped out with Tyler as much as she did. But Rita needed to get it together, she had her child to think about.

"I need you to get off this case right now."

"I'm in my car, Rita. The guy doesn't even know that I'm here." Just as she said that Jason stood up and stretched. The roofer guy stood up also. She really needed to get off this call so she could do her job. "Why are you so upset?"

"Your job just makes me nervous. I don't know how you can do this. If something happens to you, there will be no one to help me raise Tyler. Is that what you want?"

"Calm down, okay? I'm just doing my job. Nothing is going to happen to me."

"I feel it in my gut, Britney. Something bad is about to happen. I want you to stop whatever you're doing and get out of there immediately."

"I've got to finish my work. But I'll come by to pick up Tyler and take her to the park when I'm done."

"No! Listen to me, Britney. It was during my prayer time. I closed my eyes and began to meditate and then God showed me a vision of someone lying on the floor, dead. I couldn't make out who it was, so I'm not taking any chances. Get here now."

The roofer guy walked around to the front of the house. Jason picked up a hammer from the tool box on the back patio and headed for the ladder. "I'm a big girl, Rita. I can take care of myself. I'll talk to you later." She hung up the phone, picked up her camera and rolled down her window.

Jason stood by the ladder, but before getting on he turned around and looked directly at Britney's car. "Busted. Oh God, please don't let Jason kill me and have Rita be right about this," she said as she laid her camera down and turned the ignition key. But as she was about to pull off, Jason turned away from her and started climbing the ladder. She picked the camera back up and snapped several shots of him on the ladder and on the roof. She drove around the block. When she came back around to Jason's house he was slinging that hammer like a pro. Britney snapped a couple shots of that and then drove off. Mission accomplished without anybody getting dead.

As she rounded the corner her phone rang again. She picked up her cell phone, pressed the phone button and then said, "I left already. Nobody is dead, okay, Rita." Her friend's premonition almost cost her the money shot that she had been waiting two weeks to get. Britney had gotten scared when Jason looked at her car. She began to fear for her life, all because of what Rita had said. She needed to have a serious talk with her, and soon.

"This isn't Rita. It's RaShawn."

Britney took the phone away from her ear and looked at the caller ID. RaShawn Thomas was a Morris Chestnut kind of fine bishop in Washington, D.C. who had once saved her life. She owed him big time. So far, all she'd been able to do was treat him to dinner once or twice a year. "What's up, Bishop? Don't tell me, you're calling to weasel out of dinner, aren't you?" Britney's uncle Tony had asked her to join him for breakfast on Saturday. Since she had to be in Washington, Britney had invited her favorite bishop in the whole wide world to dinner.

"Of course not, I want to have dinner with you very much," RaShawn said.

"That's good. So, what's going on?"

He hesitated. "I-I have some bad news for you."

"Did all your pastors quit on you or something?" RaShawn presided over seventeen churches, including her uncle's church. Tony Hartman was not happy to answer to a thirty-seven-year-old bishop. But, if he wanted to keep his church he had to roll with it. Britney found the whole situation amusing; thus her joke about all the pastors quitting.

"It's much worse than that, Britney. I just left your uncle's house." He hesitated again. "I really hate to tell you this, but I think your mother would rather get this news from you than from me."

Britney pulled up to a red light. "Will you just tell me what's going on already?"

"I'm so sorry, Britney, but Tony is dead."

A car horn honked behind her. Britney looked up and saw that the light had turned green. But for a moment she couldn't seem to press the pedal. "What did you say?"

The horn honked again.

Britney drove off, but at the next block she pulled her car over to the side of the road.

"Tony is dead, Britney. I found him lying on the floor in his home office."

"Good Lord, what happened?"

"The police think he was poisoned. I'm really sorry to unload all of this on you. I should have called your mom, but I knew she wouldn't want to speak to me."

"Don't worry about it, RaShawn. Thank you for calling. I'll let mom know." As Britney hung up the phone she thought back to Rita's words about seeing someone lying on the floor dead. Maybe that girl really was having premonitions. As much as Britney wanted Rita to be wrong, she knew that she would find no joy in being right. Not this time.

Chapter Three

RaShawn was having a hard time dealing with the death of Tony Hartman. As he sat in the church watching mourners pay their respects, all he could think was that it was his fault that Tony was dead. He wondered who was next, and if the police would really be able to stop this madman.

The church was overflowing with people from all walks of life. Tony had been a very charismatic and respected minister. His Christian broadcast was viewed by hundreds of thousands. He and his ex-wife had even done a reality show which had been viewed by millions who gleefully tuned in each week to see the implosion of Tony and Carla Hartman's twenty-year marriage.

Carla had wanted nothing else to do with Tony after the divorce, which was the reason RaShawn chose to call Britney. He figured that she and her mother could sort out the rest of the people who needed to be contacted. But as he looked down at the front row and witnessed how Tony and Carla's two teenage sons held on so tightly to their mother as she wept, he realized he'd made a mistake. He should have driven over to Carla's home and told her the news in person.

Carla had divorced Tony because she'd lost respect for him as a man of God and a husband, but that obviously hadn't stopped her from holding love in her heart for the man who'd had countless affairs while married to her. His heart went out to Carla and every woman who'd ever married a man and expected happily-ever-after, but received heartache and tears instead.

As he was leaving the grave yard, Judge Hartman and Britney, he greeted them with a hug and offered his condolences once again.

Britney said, "Uncle Tony was a good man; I just don't understand this at all. But I guarantee that I will find out who did this to him."

"Don't waste your time on this investigation." Judge Hartman pointed an accusatory finger at RaShawn as she said, "Just ask the good bishop here who he thinks is responsible for Tony's death."

RaShawn was drained. He didn't understand what God was doing or why any of this was happening on his watch. He understood that Judge Hartman blamed him, but he wasn't in the mood for arguing the point. "I need to get home. I'll talk to you all another time."

As RaShawn walked away from them he was wondering if he'd truly heard from God when he took this job and was seriously thinking about resigning and letting someone else take over as bishop. Maybe his approach had been too heavy handed… who was he to judge whether anyone was fit to stand behind a pulpit or not?

RaShawn was a grown man, well into his thirties, but after the day he'd just endured, he needed his stepmother and his father. So, he threw a few clothes in an overnight bag, hopped in his car and drove to Raleigh, NC.

***

Carmella Marshall-Thomas was in the kitchen putting the finishing touches on the dinner she was making to celebrate the fact that RaShawn was coming home for the weekend. Her husband's youngest son had moved back to the states after spending years on the mission field. But his schedule was so busy that he didn't make it home as much as Carmella would have liked. So, when he called and said that he was coming to see them, Carmella ran to the grocery store and was now throwing together a dinner party for her family. Joy and Renee still lived in Raleigh, so they were helping her with dinner.

"Remember how you used to hate helping out in the kitchen," Joy said as she nudged Renee. "You used to make me and Raven so mad."

"It took me a while to get used to you and Mama-Carmella. But I'm in here with you now. And besides, Jay loves all the recipes and tips I get from Mama-Carmella."

"Oh, so you're just using us to keep your gorgeous husband's stomach full?"

Renee laughed. "Shut up, Joy. You're just trying to project your sins on me. We all know you come here to get recipes from Mama-Carmella for your handsome husband. In case you've forgotten, I've heard Lance brag about the veggie lasagna recipe that you got out of the same kitchen I got it from."

"Okay ladies, your brother is almost here so we don't have time for fighting. Let's just say that both of you steal my recipes, and I love it." She hugged both her daughters and then said, "Now help me take all this food that you part-time chefs helped to create, to the dining room table."

Ronny had mended from his car accident, so he and his wife, Nia, were no longer staying with them. Carmella missed them like nobody's business, but her children were all grown now, and she and Ramsey had to step back and let them live their lives. But she wasn't complaining. They now had five grandchildren to spoil. She and Ramsey had just booked a five-night Disney cruise for the grands.

Joy went to the cabinet and pulled out the best china that her mother always used when serving her family. It didn't have to be Thanksgiving or Christmas, because Carmella was thankful to God for every chance she had to spend with her family. "I've got the plates," Joy told them as she walked out of the kitchen.

Renee opened the drawers and pulled out the heavy silverware. As she headed to the dining room, she told Carmella, "I know that you love your family. But if they come to my house for dinner, I'm giving these messy kids paper plates and plasticware."

"We only have one of the grandkids with us today, I think she can handle the china." Carmella picked up the bowl of salad and rolls, and headed out to the table with them.

"You want to give the grandkids china, fine. But I beg you, give RaShawn a paper plate. That boy is worse than the kids."

***

As RaShawn pulled up in his parents' driveway, he leaned back in his seat as he pulled the key out of the ignition and breathed a sigh of relief. He was out of his element as bishop. Why he ever thought that he could make a difference was beyond his understanding. So far, all he'd managed to do was cause the deaths of three pastors within his ministry.

"What are you doing sitting out in this car when we're all in here waiting on you so we can eat dinner?" Ramsey asked his son as he held the front door open.

This was home, this was where he could be himself. He wasn't the bishop of twenty churches here, he was just RaShawn. And he was late for dinner. "I'm coming, Dad."

RaShawn got out of his car and went inside to greet his family. Once inside he spotted the dining table with its mounds and mounds of food. His stepmother never did anything halfway. But through the years she'd learned that cooking healthy food was better for her family, so the table was graced with baked chicken, salmon, asparagus, spinach and sweet potato home fries.

"Why didn't you all wait for me? I could have helped out in the kitchen, you know." During RaShawn's years on the mission field he'd learned to cook and didn't mind showing off his culinary skills.

"You had to drive all the way here. I didn't want you to worry about fixing your own meal as well," Carmella told him as she placed the last dish on the table. "Now, let's eat."

The family sat down for food, conversation and good-natured fun. The Marshall-Thomas family truly enjoyed being around one another. If anything, Carmella and

Ramsey could write a book on successful blended families. It was because their families were so well blended that Joy and Dontae thought of Ramsey's kids as brothers and sisters, no "step" included.

""You did your thing on this meal. I'm full and still want seconds," Jay said to his mother-in-law.

"Hey," Renee objected. "I helped out in the kitchen. How do you know *I* didn't fix one of the items you're oohing and aaahing over?"

"No offense, hon, but you've never fixed sweet potatoes like this. I didn't even know they could be made to taste just as good as an Idaho potato," Jay said while gently placing a hand over his wife's arm.

Smiling, Renee told him, "I got the recipe, so you'll be seeing those potatoes on our table soon enough, buster."

Joy pointed an accusatory finger at Renee. "See Mama, I told you she was only helping so that she could impress Jay with her culinary skills."

"Leave her alone, Joy. I already told you that both of you are welcome to any recipe that I have."

Renee stuck out her tongue at her sister and everyone at the table laughed... everyone except RaShawn, who had so much on his mind that he couldn't even enjoy a moment of fun with his family.

"What's eating at you, son?" Carmella asked as everyone settled in the family room.

Hanging his head, RaShawn apologized for bringing the mood down. "Maybe I shouldn't have come."

Renee sat down next to her brother and put her arm around him. "You have nothing to be sorry about. We should be apologizing to you. Here we are carrying on, joking about trivial things while you're dealing with these horrible things happening to the preachers in your fellowship."

He waved off her concern as his shoulders slumped. "I don't want to burden anyone with my problems. I just needed to get away from them so I can clear my head and figure out what I need to do."

"I hope you're not blaming yourself for all of this craziness," Joy said as she sat down on his right side and joined Renee in comforting her brother.

"How can I not?" RaShawn shook his head like he was trying to shake the guilt away from his very presence. "Those men died because I exposed their sins. If I had just left them alone and not fired them, none of this would be happening."

Putting her hands on her hips in righteous indignation, Carmella stood up. "RaShawn Thomas, you can't honestly be blaming yourself for the way those men lived their lives." Closing her eyes and taking a deep breath, she added, "May God rest their souls because I pray that each one of them had time to repent of their sins. But I had stopped watching their TV ministries years ago. The Lord had revealed to me that they were no longer in the faith."

"You knew?" His stepmother's godly wisdom amazed him. She always seemed to know when any of them needed prayer or a word of encouragement. Now she was telling them that she could even spot God frauds… that was what RaShawn called them. In general a God fraud was a preacher who didn't live what he preached.

Carmella nodded. "Believe it or not, God marks those who belong to Him. And those preachers had lost the glow that the anointing puts on every believer. They were still standing behind the pulpit and preaching to millions, but I knew something had gone wrong, because I could see that they didn't believe in what they preached anymore."

"So don't you be down on yourself," Ramsey told his son. "God calls each and every one of us to holiness. And if the preacher can't live up to those standards, how in the world is he going to teach anyone else to live holy?"

RaShawn knew what they were saying was true. In his head he knew that he hadn't caused the deaths of those preachers, their shady living had ruined their relationships with God and man. But his heart was asking why he hadn't just given them another chance.

Standing up, RaShawn told the group, "I'm drained. Do you mind if I take my old room and lay down for a little while?"

"Of course not. I put everything you need in there right after you called," Carmella told him.

"Thanks," RaShawn said as he walked away from the group with his head down. When he reached his old room, he threw his bag on the dresser and then jumped in the bed, put his face in the pillow and prayed that sleep would come quickly so he wouldn't have to think about the lives he'd destroyed with his live-right edict.

Chapter Four

RaShawn wanted to sleep so he could close his mind to the trauma he'd been dealing with. But all through the night images of the men whom he'd deemed unfit to stand behind a pulpit chased him while he tried to sleep. They were reaching out to him, begging him to help them. RaShawn screamed at Tony Hartman, "I can't help you. You're already dead."

"Then help me."

RaShawn swung around to face Pastor Marvel Williams. This man of God who supposedly believed every word in the Bible had, just two weeks ago, performed a wedding ceremony for his son and his son's male lover. When RaShawn asked how he could justify what he had done to the kingdom of God, Pastor Marvel had shrugged as he said, "He's my son. I was just showing him unconditional love."

Shaking his head, RaShawn told the man, "No one can fault you for loving your son. If I had a son and he fell into the sin of homosexuality, that wouldn't change the love I have in my heart for him. But what I wouldn't do is condone his sin by standing in a pulpit that belongs to God and marry him off to something he never should have been connected with in the first place."

Then Pastor Marvel stood up and boldly declared, "I don't preach against homosexuality in my pulpit because no one has ever shown me where God speaks against it in the Bible."

Holy indignation rose up in RaShawn at the pastor's words. "You must not be reading your Bible if you don't know that this thing simply shouldn't be done. But I'll give you a quick Bible lesson if I must. Why don't you read Leviticus 20:13 where it says, "If a man lies with a male as he lies with a woman, both of them have committed an abomination?

"If that isn't clear enough for you, then flip backward to Genesis chapter 19 and read all about how God destroyed Sodom and Gomorrah because the men wanted to sleep with other men. Try opening your Bible to Romans 1:26-27, and then tell me that God hasn't said that homosexuality is wrong.

"Many people think that God is an ever changing God and that those scriptures of old no longer relate to this modern world," Marvel had said, still trying to justify his actions.

"God is the same yesterday, today and forever. Holiness is what he has always required." RaShawn stood with sadness in his eyes. He looked down on Marvel and said, "I will not debate the word of God with someone who is supposed to be preaching it. I want you to clear out your office. You have preached your last sermon for this fellowship."

At the time RaShawn had been so angry that he just wanted Marvel out of his sight and to never have to deal with the man again. But as he tossed and turned and Marvel's face kept appearing to him, RaShawn bolted upright in bed. He was drenched in sweat as he frantically searched the room for the faces that had creeped into his nightmare.

"Was I wrong, Lord? Did you have something else in mind for Marvel?"

No answer came to him at that moment. But Marvel hadn't been murdered like some of the other pastors that he'd fired. Hopefully, he would have time to figure out God's perfect will as it related to that situation before it was too late.

He got out of bed, took a shower and then headed for the kitchen where wonderful smells of eggs and turkey bacon were drifting toward him. Mama-Carmella was flipping pancakes and dancing around the kitchen as a praise song blared through the overhead speakers.

"I thought you stopped eating pancakes." RaShawn said as he stepped into the kitchen.

"Gluten free, my boy. These pancakes are made with bananas, almond meal and flax seed."

"You are a miracle worker in the kitchen, Mama-Carmella. I wish I still lived here so you could feed me every day."

Smiling at him she said, "You might have a hard time finding a wife if you become a big old mama's boy."

"With the way things have been going, I'm not sure that any woman would want me. I've been told that I'm too judgmental, in case you haven't heard."

Carmella turned off the stove. She walked over to RaShawn, kissed his forehead and then sat down next to him. She took his hands and held them tight. "I know you're dealing with a lot right now. But I don't ever want you to forget that you haven't asked these pastors for anything more than what God requires of us all... that we should live holy."

"I know. But I feel like I'm way out of my league with everything that's going on. If I didn't have this revival coming up next week, I'd probably stay here and hide out. I need some time to figure out what God is doing."

As she released his hands, Carmella said, "Listen to you. Son, don't you know who you are? God has given you the ability to cast out demons. I might not have been there, but your sister was a witness to it, so you can't deny that the power of God works mightily in you. Now God has elevated you to the office of a bishop. Trust Him, He knows what he's doing."

He wanted to just trust God and not give a second thought to all the other circumstances swirling around him that seemed to scream... *out of your league*. But he felt as if he was just as weak and on the run as Elijah had been when Queen Jezebel had threatened his life.

Tamela Mann's song, "I Can Only Imagine" came on the radio. Carmella popped up and praise danced over to the stove. "Let me get you some breakfast," she said, still dancing as she grabbed the spatula.

Watching his stepmother dance across the floor as if she were truly in the presence of the King and imagining what He would have to say to her, brought a smile to RaShawn's face. As Carmella put his breakfast in front of him and then danced back around to her seat, he told her,

"I wish I could dance and praise the Lord the way you do. But I've got two left feet when it comes to dancing."

"You don't have to get up and dance across the floor. Living holy is your song of praise, RaShawn Thomas. And believe me, it is so very acceptable to God."

The beginnings of a smile stretched across RaShawn's face. It was the first time he'd smiled in weeks. He opened his mouth to thank Carmella for giving him something to smile about but his cell rang. He looked down, and fear clenched his heart when he saw that the call was coming from Detective Harris.

"What's wrong?" Carmella asked when she saw the stricken look on his face.

"I hope nothing," RaShawn said as he answered his phone and then listened to everything Detective Harris had to say. When he ended the call, RaShawn turned to Carmella. "I won't be staying for breakfast. Another pastor within my fellowship is dead. I need to get back home."

***

Pastor Darnel King had been preaching the gospel for ten years. With over five thousand members, his ministry was flowing and RaShawn was always blessed whenever he was able to sit in on one of Pastor King's dynamic messages. Being that Pastor King was only a few years older than he, RaShawn had hoped that the two of them would become great friends. Pastor Darnel King was not one of the six pastors he had recently fired, and therefore, RaShawn was baffled by his untimely death.

"I don't get it, Jarod, I mean, Darnel King was one of the good guys. And I certainly didn't fire him, so why is he dead?"

"That's not the only problem with this kill." Jarod shook his head. "His wife was hysterical when we arrived at the house, said that she found her husband on the floor when she came home from a shopping trip. But there was no note, and no grape juice. I asked if she'd taken anything out of the room." Jarod shrugged, "She said she didn't."

RaShawn plopped down. "The press never reported anything about the note this Avenger leaves behind. And the only reason I knew anything about the grape juice was because I arrived at Tony Hartman's house before you did."

"Exactly," Jarod said, as if RaShawn was catching his point. "Pastor King's body has no visible signs of stab wounds or gun shots, so I told Mrs. King that we would have to do an autopsy. She went all types of crazy then. Claimed we were trying to desecrate her husband's body. She said she wouldn't allow it. But I told her that since her husband died under suspicious circumstances, there was going to be an autopsy."

"You can't honestly think that Vicki King had anything to do with Darnel's death? The woman adored her husband."

"The coroner worked overtime on this one. The report came in this morning, that's why I called you."

"And?"

Jarod stood up and grabbed his keys. "I need to ride out to the widow's house. I was hoping you'd come with me. She might be more forthcoming with you by her side."

"Of course I'll come with you. But what did the autopsy show? Was there any grape juice in Darnel's system?"

"It wasn't grape juice. Come on, I'll explain everything in the car on the way over there. But I'm telling you now… you're not going to believe this one."

Jarod had been right. As RaShawn sat next to Vicki King, he was still trying to wrap his head around the coroner's findings.

Jarod sat across from them and put his cards on the table. "The autopsy is not complete, but the coroner discovered something so disturbing that she contacted me first thing this morning."

RaShawn kept his eyes on Vicki, trying to determine if she looked any different to him now than she had when he'd seen her a few weeks ago. He could only see the grief-stricken face in front of him, but he couldn't see inside of her to know whether or not she was capable of plotting to kill a man, then setting out on a task that had taken weeks, if not months to accomplish.

"The coroner found glass in your husband's stomach."

Turning to RaShawn for help, Vicki said, "What about this man who's going around killing preachers? Maybe he made Darnel eat glass."

Jarod shook his head. "According the initial findings, Pastor King has been eating glass for a few months. The coroner thinks it was ground up in his food."

Vicki leaned back in her seat, crossed her arms around her chest, but she didn't respond.

"Do you know how something like this could have happened?" Jarod asked, after enduring a long silence.

Vicki shrugged, grief disappearing from her face as a shadow of something RaShawn didn't recognize took its place. "I don't know. Maybe he liked glass, like those weirdos who sniff glue."

"The glass was ground up so the police think someone put the glass in Darnel's food. Don't you have a housekeeper?" RaShawn asked, trying to nudge Vicki to say something helpful before Jarod slapped the cuffs on her.

"No, I fired her a few months ago." Tears flowed down Vicki's face as she added, "My wonderful husband was sleeping with her."

"W-wait… wh-what are you talking about?" RaShawn felt as if he was having one of those dreams where he was falling and falling and falling. This couldn't be real. Darnel King was one of the first pastors to reach out to him when he took over as bishop. They were becoming friends. The man was honorable and Godly.

"Does that surprise you?" Vicki turned to RaShawn. A bitter laugh escaped as she said, "I thought for sure you'd see it. But you were so enamored by Darnel's preaching style that you never bothered to look any deeper."

Defending himself, RaShawn said, "I researched all of the pastors within my fellowship. No one had a bad word to say about Darnel."

"That was because his secretary steered you in the direction she wanted you to go. She's been sleeping with Darnel for over five years and treats me like an insect every time I come to the office. He allowed all of his women to treat me like that." Vicki lowered her head and cried like her heart had been broken.

RaShawn put an arm around her shoulder, trying to comfort her. He'd had no idea what Vicki had endured all of these years. He silently prayed that Darnel's actions hadn't destroyed Vicki's relationship with God.

Jarod leaned forward as he gently asked, "Did you feed Pastor King the glass?"

Sorrow etched her tone as she told them, "Darnel loved having a bunch of women. But he never trusted any of them to cook for him... that was my job." Looking Jarod square in the eye, Vicki said, "I'd like to call my lawyer."

Chapter Five

Reporters were hogging the steps of the church when RaShawn arrived. They threw microphones in his face and hurled questions at him as he tried to get inside the church.

"Why are the pastors in this town being murdered?"

RaShawn swatted a microphone out of his face and kept walking.

"We have it on good authority that you fired three of the dead preachers. Do you think someone is exacting their own brand of judgment on these men?"

"I can't comment on an ongoing investigation. You all need to go to the police station and ask your questions." RaShawn had his hand on the door to the church. He was almost in the building.

"Were these men sinners? Is that why they were killed?"

What did these reporters want from him? Did they expect him to list each of the dirty deeds committed by these so-called preachers for the nightly news? RaShawn opened the door and quickly made his way into the church.

Thankfully, the reporters had enough respect not to follow him.

His secretary greeted him with a stack of phone messages. "I'm glad you're back. The phone has been ringing off the hook. Our members are threatening to find other churches to attend or to not go to church at all."

That didn't make sense to RaShawn. None of the killings occurred at church. "I hope you assured them that the church is the same safe haven it's always been."

"I tried. But some of them still want their membership back."

"Okay, well, I guess I'll get on the phone and try to reassure our members that this is a safe place to attend church."

"One more thing that you're not going to like." She handed him another note. "Minister Donald Hayward cancelled."

RaShawn was about to explode. "What do you mean, he cancelled. The revival is this weekend. How can he just cancel three days before an event?"

Shaking her head, his secretary told him, "He told me to tell you how sorry he is about this, but that he likes living too much to tempt fate by coming here at a time like this."

Right now, RaShawn needed some prayer time... needed to ask the Lord what to do next, which way to turn. But most of all RaShawn wanted time to ask the Lord how he had gotten it all wrong. All of his life, he had only strived to do what was good and right and acceptable in the sight of God. He'd thought that getting rid of those preachers and then bringing in some new, on-fire-for-the-Lord kind of preachers was the answer to this fellowship's sin problem. But he just didn't know anymore. Maybe he should fire himself.

"Oh, I almost forgot. Britney Hartman is here. I told her to wait in your office. I hope that was okay."

No, it isn't okay, he wanted to scream at his secretary. He'd had a bear of a day and it wasn't even noon yet. He needed his prayer time like he needed to breathe. The last thing he wanted to do was look Britney Hartman in the face and have her accuse him of being the reason her uncle was dead. But instead of running away from the situation, he took a deep breath and opened the door to his office and put a smile on his face.

"You look awful," Britney said as RaShawn stepped into his office. She was seated on the sofa next to the big picture window.

"Thanks, just what I need... a good friend to tell me the truth about myself.

"I know it's been a tough morning, but you're handling it well."

RaShawn pointed towards the window. "You saw the mob scene out there?"

Nodding, Britney stood up and walked over to RaShawn's desk. As RaShawn took his jacket off and sat down, she said, "I know it's annoying to have so many people coming at you with questions that you can't answer, and I'm sorry to have to do this to you, but that's why I'm here also."

Please don't accuse me of killing Tony, please don't accuse me of killing Tony, he silently chanted to himself. RaShawn could deal with Judge Hartman believing that RaShawn was responsible for her brother-in-law's death. That woman didn't like him much anyway. She hadn't cared much for the entire Thomas family ever since she hired Raven to find Britney, and then Raven actually did her job. The problem for Judge Hartman had been that Britney had been mixed up in the scandal of Senator Allen's death and it had been an election year.

Judge Hartman had been re-elected. But she still hadn't forgiven Raven, RaShawn or her own daughter for that matter. RaShawn only prayed that Judge Hartman's brand of Christianity hadn't spread over to Britney. "I don't think this is a good time for us to talk about this, Britney. Would it be possible for you to come back another day?"

She shook her head. "I've taken a leave of absence from my job, but I can't stay away indefinitely, or I'll have to find another way to pay my bills."

RaShawn was proud of Britney. She'd been through some very trying times, but despite it all, she managed to pull herself up and turn her life around. RaShawn knew how important her career was to her, and if she had taken a leave of absence, then he needed to make time for her. The last thing he wanted was for Tony's death to be the cause of a major setback. "Have a seat, Britney. Of course I can make time for you."

"Thank you so much, Bishop Thomas."

RaShawn held up a hand. "I told you before. It's just RaShawn to you." From the moment RaShawn laid eyes on Britney in that godawful place the senator's wife had lured her to, he knew that they were destined to meet and destined to become great friends.

"Of course you told me that," Britney said, smiling at him, "But that was before you became a bishop. Now I'm all worried about offending you if I don't use your title."

"The only way I'll be offended is if you persist in calling me bishop. Now what can I do for you?"

"Okay, RaShawn… I'm here because I need your help. I know you and my uncle didn't see eye to eye, but he was a good man. My father passed away when I was just three years old. Then my mother married my awful stepfather. To this day, I still don't believe that she didn't know that he had a thing for little girls." Britney closed her eyes, trying to block out unwanted memories. Shaking herself, she continued, "Anyway, my visits with my uncle were the only thing that kept me from killing myself back then.

"One summer, I was so despondent from the things I had endured at my mother's house that Uncle Tony made me tell him what was going on." A big smile crossed her face as she thought about that summer. "I don't know what he did, but by the time I went back home, my twisted stepfather had moved out of the house and my uncle assured me that I would never have to see that man again in life."

RaShawn washed down the huge lump in his throat. Just knowing that Tony had compassion for Britney all those years ago made RaShawn wish he had taken the time to get to know Tony before he'd dismissed him.

But RaShawn had been in a rush to be the battle axe God had called him to be. Now he wondered if God was pleased with the way he was running this fellowship. "I'm sorry that I didn't give him a chance," was all he could say to Britney.

"I'm not saying that you didn't have cause to fire him. He never should have gone into the ministry if he wasn't going to be faithful to his wife."

"You knew about that?"

She nodded. "My aunt used to cry herself to sleep. I never understood why she stayed, and then one day it became too much for her."

"I could have understood if my aunt had gone wacko one night and then shot him. But to have Uncle Tony die like this... at the hands of someone killing preachers because of the sin in their lives... I just can't wrap my mind around that."

"What makes you think they were killed because of sin?" That information hadn't been released to the media, although some had begun speculating.

"It just stands to reason. Anyway, I know all of the men you fired. They each used to attend meetings at my wonderful mother's house. They all professed to know God, but couldn't seem to get out of sin's way."

Her assessment was right. Pastor Curtis, the first preacher he fired was a known gambler who had embezzled a million dollars from his church's building fund. If the Avenger hadn't murdered him, Pastor Curtis would have spent at least ten years in prison. The list of misdeeds were long for all six of the men he'd let go. But not one of them had willingly agreed to step down. The power received from their positions was more important to them than being right with God. Maybe that was the thing that bothered this Avenger... maybe that was the reason he had communion with them. To cleanse their souls.

"Doesn't this bother you?" Britney asked. "Don't you want to know who has set himself up as God and decided to kill these men, rather than allow them time to repent?"

"Of course it bothers me. The maniac has been sending emails to me as if I'm cheering him on or something. I want to stop him before he gets to the next pastor on his list. But I don't know what to do other than wait on the police to find this guy."

Britney waved that notion away. "We don't have to wait on the police. I'm a trained investigator. Work with me, RaShawn and I promise you, we will find this guy."

Chapter Six

RaShawn didn't know if he'd agreed to work with Britney because she was an experienced researcher or because he wanted to be around her... keep a close eye on her and ensure that Tony's death didn't cause her to spiral backward. She'd come a long way, and he wasn't going to let anything get in her way, not on his watch.

Britney scooted her chair close to RaShawn's desk. She took out a notepad and pen. "Okay, we don't have much time, so let's get going. How many preachers have you fired since you took office?"

"Six."

"And three are already dead." She jotted something on her tablet then asked, "Did they die in order?"

A puzzled look appeared on RaShawn's face. "In order? What do you mean?"

"Who did you fire first, second and third?"

"Oh," RaShawn said as he gathered his thoughts. "I just thought this guy was taking vengeance on each of them because of the things they had done. But now that you mention it, my first meeting was with Charles, then Mike and then Tony."

"How would this vigilante know the reason you fired each preacher?"

"As far as I was told, no one else knew what was going on. The senior bishop handed me files on each of the pastors within my fellowship. He told me that the information in those files hadn't been shared with anyone else... well, except the members of the board."

"In what order did you fire the next three pastors?"

RaShawn opened a file, reviewed it and then said, "I let Daniel Marson go, then Lucas Linden and then Marvel Williams."

"And you've already given the police their names, right?"

"Of course. Detective Harris has also provided protection for each one of them. I'm praying that they stay alive and that the police catch this crazed person before he can do anymore harm."

"I bet you never imagined how tough being the hatchet man would be, huh?"

RaShawn leaned back in his seat, he looked heavenward, hoping to draw strength from his savior. But he felt drained and in over his head as he answered Britney. "I didn't want to be a hatchet man. All I ever wanted to do was make a difference in the kingdom. But everywhere I turn all I see is people making choices that will only lead them straight to hell. This world doesn't seem to believe that there are consequences for sin anymore, but I believe it."

"I believe it, too. Thanks to you and your sister. Everything didn't turn out the way I expected it to, but

God has been good to me. He's changed my life and I'll never turn back from serving Him."

Pointing at her, RaShawn said, "Your statement proves my point. You were willing to give God a chance to change your life because of the Christ that was presented to you. The preachers that I fired were terrible representations of Jesus Christ. And I know that you loved your uncle, but I couldn't let him stand behind that pulpit, not with an unrepentant heart… there were just too many lives at stake."

There was a loud banging on his office door and then it swung open. His secretary rushed in behind the angry man that was now glaring at RaShawn. "I'm sorry about this, Bishop. I tried to tell Pastor Linden that you were in a meeting, but he wouldn't listen."

Standing, RaShawn assured her, "It's okay. I'll take care of this. He then turned back to Linden, RaShawn refused to associate the word "pastor" with the man. He had fired him and he prayed to God that no one else was foolish enough to entrust leadership of God's house to him again. "What do you want, Linden?"

"I want you to call off the dogs," he huffed, nostrils flaring.

"What dogs? What are you talking about?"

"The cops are watching me. I know you have something to do with this. And I'm not going to put up with this type of harassment."

Shaking his head, RaShawn told him. "No one is trying to harass you. I asked Detective Harris to look out for you, Marson and Williams because I'm concerned for your safety."

"You called me a thief, accused me of furnishing my house with the church building fund. You turned me in to the police, and I have to face a judge tomorrow morning to defend myself against baseless charges. So I don't need your so-called concern. You can keep it. And if those police officers don't stop harassing me due to your unfounded accusations, I will personally contact the chief of police and let him know what you're up to."

"I'm not up to anything. I just don't want you to end up dead."

"Oh I'm more than capable of taking care of myself, as you will see if you try to come anywhere near me."

Walking toward the man, RaShawn tried to reason with him. "I have your best interest at heart here, Linden. The best advice I can give you is to let those officers do their job."

He pointed his index finger at RaShawn while holding his thumb up as if it were a gun. "And the best advice I can give you is to stay away from me so that you can live a long and fruitful life. I'm not going to be as easy a prey as the others were."

"Whoa. Did you just threaten the bishop in front of a witness?" Britney tried to keep her mouth shut and just observe as she'd been taught when handling investigations. But her mouth had flown open and words just fell out after Linden threatened RaShawn.

Linden swung around as if just taking notice of Britney's presence, even though the secretary had informed him that Bishop RaShawn was in a meeting. He had been too red-hot mad to think rationally. Backing up a bit, he said, "I didn't threaten him. It'll be my word against the both of yours if this thing goes out of this room." Linden turned on his heel getting ready to leave.

"Wait, Linden, there's something you don't know," RaShawn shouted, hoping to talk some sense into the man.

"If the information has to come from you, then I'll never know it. Just leave me alone." With that, Linden stormed out the same way he'd stormed in.

"You just can't help some people," Britney said, trying to lighten the mood.

***

All Lucas Linden wanted was to be left alone. He didn't need nor did he want help from Bishop RaShawn. The man was only trying to assuage the guilt he felt for ruining his career. Well, Linden wasn't going to soothe his conscience. Linden only hoped that the guilt would eat RaShawn Thomas alive. But if it didn't, then Linden would just have to kill the man himself.

Yes, he knew that the Bible spoke of vengeance belonging to God and that he was supposed to let God repay his enemies, but Linden didn't feel like waiting around for God to take care of a puny little insect like RaShawn Thomas.

And as he pulled up to his house he saw the police car once again. Linden didn't get mad this time... no, it was time to get even. He strolled over to the police car and said, "Hello officers, I see that you just ignored my request."

"Not true, Pastor Linden. I went back to the precinct and told my boss that you didn't want us here. I wanted to respect your wishes, but he sent me back."

"Don't you worry about it. I'm calling the chief of police because Bishop Thomas has hoodwinked all of you."

"I don't know anything about Bishop Thomas. The person who assigned me to you was Detective Harris. I can give you his number, if you'd like to complain."

"I already told you that I'm going to call the chief. I'm going to let him know how you sit out here harassing me rather than checking on Bishop Thomas' alibi during those murders. I know for a fact that Bishop Thomas killed those other preachers. He hates us, and won't stop until we're all dead."

When the police officer didn't respond, Linden shook his fist at the man and screamed in his face, "I want you out of here. Go park your car in front of Bishop Thomas' house. Make sure he stays in his house and then I'll be safe."

Angry that the officer kept ignoring him, Linden kicked the police car. "I said get out of here."

The police officer was getting angry now. He opened his door, ready to let Linden have it with some good old handcuffs and a trip downtown, but dispatch was calling out for all available units on a crime in progress just a block away from his current location. He slammed his door shut, turned on the car and then told Linden, "You are on your own." The police officer then sped off.

"Good." Linden said as he strutted towards his front door. He had already paid a vigilante group to smuggle him out of the country and make it look like this psycho killer had gotten hold of him. Linden didn't plan on showing up for court tomorrow morning and he didn't need some cop outside his front door messing everything up. With a wicked grin on his face, Linden thought to himself, *this night was nobody's business but his own.*

But as he opened his door and stepped into the house, Linden was surprised to see a bottle of wine with two glasses on his dining room table. That wasn't there when he left the house earlier today. His housekeeper was off today so he knew that she didn't do it. "Who's in here?" he barked.

"I've been waiting for you," The Avenger said, coming into view.

Linden's eyes bucked. "How did you get in here?"

The Avenger pointed towards the back of the house. "You left the patio door open."

Glancing out the front window, Linden hoped that the cop had circled around the block and was now back in front of his house.

"No one is out there, Linden. It's just you and me."

"What do you want?"

"For you to repent. That's all I've ever wanted."

Chapter Seven

"How is it that you are the one person who knows about these killings, even before the police have been called to the scene?" Britney asked. She and RaShawn had spent another hour in his office after ex-pastor Linden had stormed out. She was determined to find out who had such a grudge against her uncle that they had to kill him.

"The killer calls himself the Avenger of Sins. He has emailed me after each death." A haunted look crossed RaShawn's face as he added, "Then, either I or the police have found the body."

"Were all three of them poisoned?"

RaShawn's eyes darted toward Britney. The expression of shock was noted so Britney said, "I know that my uncle was poisoned, so I just wondered if the killer used the same method on each of the other victims."

"How do you know that? The coroner hasn't released the findings yet."

"I figured they were trying to keep things hush-hush, which is the reason I didn't tell my mother my suspicion about the poison. But when the hospital informed us that we couldn't see my uncle because they were worried about exposure, I knew that could only mean one thing."

Shaking his head, RaShawn told her, "You're too smart for your own good."

"It would help if I knew what kind of poison the killer is using. That way we could try to pinpoint people with access to those types of chemicals."

"The police were hoping to keep the method of the killings out of the news. I almost told Linden, but he stormed out of the office before I could get it out."

She scooted her chair closer. "So tell me. Remember, we're in this together. If you want to stop this psycho as much as I do, you can't hold back."

Hesitant for only a moment, RaShawn said, "Crackers and grape juice were on the table where your uncle was found. I think the killer puts poison in the grape juice and then has communion with them before they die."

"Communion?" Britney's eyebrows furrowed. "Why on earth would he have communion with them before killing them? And why would they entertain the thought of having communion with someone who wants to kill them?"

"I can't figure it out either," RaShawn said as he tapped his index finger on the desk.

Britney pointed to the computer. "Did you keep the emails?"

Swiveling around in his chair, RaShawn rolled over to the computer and opened his email. Turning back to Britney he said, "I've kept each email." RaShawn was about to open the folder with his saved email when an email popped into his in-basket that caused him to blink rapidly as his eyes watered. The message was from the Avenger. He hadn't even switched email addresses as if he had no fear of the police catching up with him.

"What's wrong?" Britney asked as she noticed the look of horror on his face.

In answer, RaShawn pointed toward the screen. "The Avenger has sent me another email. The subject line says: Lucas Linden." RaShawn jumped out of his seat and rushed toward his office door.

"Where are you going? Aren't you going to open the email?"

"I don't need to open it. I know what it says. I've got to get to Linden. I pray that the policeman is still guarding his house."

It took them twenty minutes to get across town. In that time, RaShawn had placed a call to Detective Harris. After four rings it went to voicemail. RaShawn hurriedly rattled off Linden's address and asked that he meet him at the house.

"Is this feeling like déjà vu all over again?" Britney asked as she held on to the door handle as RaShawn took the curve and kept driving like he was drag racing.

"I don't want to believe it. I just don't want to believe it." RaShawn pulled into Linden's driveway and was disheartened to see that the police detail was no longer there. Why had they left Linden to fend for himself? They'd better have a good reason, or RaShawn planned to stand in front of every TV camera he could find and tell the world how careless the police department was when it came to the lives of preachers.

"If the Avenger got to him, maybe we were wrong about this "order of firing" thing. Maybe the Avenger is using some other method of deciding who goes when," Britney said as they jumped out of the car and raced toward Linden's front door.

After knocking a few times with no answer, RaShawn tried the doorknob. Just as it had been at Tony's house, Linden's door was unlocked.

"I don't think we should go in. Maybe we should wait for the police."

"The police were supposed to be here watching Linden's back. I'm going in," RaShawn said, pushing the door wider.

"Okay, let's do it."

They stepped into the house. With Britney behind him, RaShawn called out to Linden. The only sound returning back to them was the sound of their footsteps on the hardwood floor. "Linden?" he tried again.

But as they rounded the corner and entered the living room, RaShawn's heart almost stopped in his chest. The man who had just been at his office ranting and raving, was now stretched out on the floor.

"Oh my God," Britney said as she moved closer to Linden. She checked his pulse, shook her head and then asked, "Is this how the others were found?"

RaShawn didn't answer and Britney didn't notice that he was standing behind her weeping. She looked over at the coffee table and noted the grape juice, crackers and one wine goblet. Still scanning the room she turned back to Linden and noticed the written note on his back, *You do right, and I won't do wrong.*

A chill went through her as she read those words. Something about that phrase bothered her. She'd heard it before... but where? When? Moving away from Linden's body she stood next to RaShawn and put her arm around him. "I'm sorry, RaShawn, I know that this is the last thing you wanted to happen."

"And yet another man is dead." RaShawn wiped the tears from his face and then helplessly stared at Linden's body. "What am I supposed to do now? How can I lead this fellowship if I am the cause of so many deaths?"

"This is not your fault, RaShawn and I'm going to help you prove it."

RaShawn didn't respond, he just kept staring at Linden.

Britney moved him over to the sofa and nudged him to sit down. "You wait here for the police, I'm going to go around back to see if there's a trail or something back there." If someone had been in the house, Britney doubted that they left through the front door. If she could find a footprint or something the killer left behind, that might be enough to get the investigation headed in the right direction.

He grabbed her arm. "Be careful. I don't know what I'd do if anything happened to you."

"I'm an investigator, RaShawn. I know how to handle myself. I'll be right back."

She walked off and RaShawn was so afraid for her that he started to get up and go after her.

"Bishop, are you in here?"

RaShawn heard Detective Harris calling out to him. He hollered back, "I'm in here." It was still daylight outside, so he figured Britney would be safe out back for a few minutes.

Jarod Harris stepped into the room, took one look at the body on the floor and called for the coroner. He then he chided RaShawn about entering another crime scene.

"I know, I know." RaShawn waved the detective's comments off. "But I wouldn't even be here if the police detail you promised was still here."

The moment he said that another police officer stormed into the room. He took one look at Linden's lifeless body and shook his head. "I knew I shouldn't have listened to that mean old goat."

"Are you the officer who was supposed to be watching out for Linden?" RaShawn demanded.

"Look, Bishop, I know you're upset. But you can save the righteous indignation, because the fact is, Linden told me that he had proof that you're the one killing these preachers. And wonder of all wonders, you show up at another crime scene."

"Okay, Carter, that's enough," Detective Harris said.

Carter swung around to face off with Harris. "No, it's not enough." Pointing toward RaShawn he said, "Our victim as much as implicated this man in his murder and within an hour he's dead. Now if you don't haul the bishop down to the station house, I'll call the chief and get the clearance to do it myself."

"You want to haul me in because you didn't do your job in the first place. That's ludicrous." RaShawn couldn't believe what he was hearing. But he was beginning to realize that he wouldn't be able to count on the police to solve this case, not if they were going to use him as a scapegoat.

"You know as well as I do that killers like coming back to the scene of the crime… they even get some sick thrill out of inserting themselves into the investigation. So, are you going to hook him up or should I?" Carter asked while holding his handcuffs.

Rolling his eyes heavenward, Harris turned to RaShawn with an apologetic look on his face. "I think you do need to come down to the station, Bishop." Harris then turned to his fellow officer. "The coroner and another investigation team are on the way, stay here until they arrive. Do you think you can do that?" The sarcasm was evident in Harris' voice.

"I got this covered. You just take your friend to the station, before we let our only suspect get away."

The tension between the two officers was palpable. RaShawn felt as though he was caught in the middle of whatever these two had against each other. Neither man was thinking logically at the moment, so RaShawn said, "Not a problem. I'll meet you at the station."

"No dice, Bishop," Carter said, still holding the handcuffs. "We wouldn't trust any other suspect that we found hovering over a dead body to meet us at the station, so you're either going in the back of my car or Harris'… take your pick."

"He's right, Bishop. I need to ask you to ride with me."

"Am I under arrest?"

Detective Harris shook his head. "Not as of now. But you will need to clear some things up before we can rule you out as a suspect."

RaShawn wished he had taken Detective Harris' advice and stayed away from the crime scenes, but he had been drawn to them like a moth to a flame. "Do you have to cuff me?"

"No. That won't be necessary. Let's just go." Harris took hold of RaShawn's arm and walked him out of the house towards his car.

When RaShawn saw Britney coming back around to the front of the house, he hurriedly told the detective, "She came here with me. She was checking out back to see if there were any tracks."

"Great, now I've got another person meddling in my crime scene. Do I need to round up all your friends too?"

"No, you're right. I shouldn't have brought her with me."

Harris stared at Britney a moment and then said, "Don't I know you? Weren't you just in my office asking questions about Pastor Hartman?"

Britney nodded. "Tony was my uncle."

RaShawn handed her his keys. "Take my SUV and give Raven a call. Tell her to alert the family that they might hear some craziness on the news, but not to worry."

"Wait, I don't understand. Where are you taking him?" Britney asked the detective.

"We're going to the precinct and unless you want to go too, I suggest you do just as the bishop suggested."

Britney backed up, but as she made her way to RaShawn's car she promised him, "I'll take care of this. You will be out of there soon." She jumped in the Range Rover and headed to the one and only place she could turn.

Chapter Eight

"What do you mean, RaShawn has been arrested?" Ramsey yelled into the phone.

"Calm down, Daddy," Raven said. "He hasn't actually been arrested, more like detained. But Marcus and I are on our way to Washington to find out what's going on. I'll let you know more once we get there."

"I guess you forgot that we're retired. You don't have to tell me nothing but where to meet up, because Carmella and I will be on the road in a matter of minutes."

"Okay, Dad, I'll call back and let you know if we were able to get RaShawn out of the police station."

"You do that," Ramsey said before hanging up. He then went into the back yard where his wife was working with the landscapers on making their back yard like one of those Yard Chaser yards. He hated taking her away from something that she was enjoying so much, but they didn't have time to waste.

"Hey, honey, I'm glad you came out here. We're trying to decide whether or not to cut down the trees on the left side of the yard."

Ramsey shook the landscaper's hand and said, "I'm sorry to have to do this, but something has come up and we need to reschedule."

The landscaper suggested, "We're making progress, if you can give us just a few more minutes, I'll be out of your way and then I can get started that much sooner."

Carmella didn't even entertain the thought of asking her husband to wait. She knew Ramsey well enough to know that he wouldn't just throw a monkey wrench in the middle of her plans unless something was very wrong. "We'll get back to you. I'll give you a call and schedule another time that's more convenient." She then walked back into the house with Ramsey. She squeezed his hand while asking, "What was that about?"

"Thanks for trusting my judgment, babe."

"Of course, now tell me what's going on." Carmella searched his eyes as if trying to read his mind.

"It's RaShawn. The police have detained him. They think he has something to do with those murders."

"Oh, it's time to go to war," Carmella declared.

"Exactly what I was thinking. Let's grab a few things and head on to Washington so we can figure this thing out."

"Just wait one minute, mister. I don't know what kind of battle you think you're going to fight without praying first, but I can guarantee it'll be a losing one. So, I'm not leaving this house until we take this matter to God."

Ramsey bent down and kissed his wife. "I thank God every day for sending you to me, Mrs. Carmella Marshall-Thomas."

They held hands and went to war.

***

Britney had not been inside her mother's house in over five years. There were too many bad memories... too many unresolved issues. But she couldn't think about that now. RaShawn needed the kind of pull her mother could provide, and Britney was going to make sure that her mother put the full weight of her judgeship behind RaShawn.

"Well, to what do I owe the pleasure of your company?" Judge Hartman asked as her daughter walked into her library.

"I don't want to be in this house any longer than necessary so I'm not going to beat around the bush. Bishop Thomas is in police custody and I need you to help those dunderheads see reason and release him."

"Has he been arrested? On what charge?" Judge Hartman seemed intrigued as she gleefully rubbed her hands together.

Plopping down on the recliner in front of the massive bookshelves, Britney sighed heavily. "I don't know why you hate Bishop Thomas so much. The man saved my life. I would think you'd thank him for that."

"Don't give me this Bishop Thomas stuff. You're in love with him. Lord only knows what the two of you do on these so-called appreciation dinners you come to town every month for."

"You know about that?" How she ever thought she could keep anything from her mother was... "How long have you known?"

"Calm down. I'm not going to tell anyone about your little affair with our hypocritical bishop."

"I'm not having an affair with RaShawn. And he is far from a hypocrite. I realize that you've spent your life with one horrible man after the next, but that doesn't mean that every man has evil intentions."

Judge Hartman visibly jerked as though being slapped by the insult. Quickly recovering she said, "Say what you want of me, but we both know who's responsible for your uncle's death."

Sighing deeply, Britney said, "You're awfully unforgiving for a woman who claims to love God."

"I'm a judge, Britney, I don't deal in forgiveness. I've been trained to interpret situations lawfully."

Why had she come here? Her mother was the meanest so-called Christian she'd ever known. To think that she would help RaShawn simply because her only child asked her to, was just not going to happen. But Britney knew how to make her mother do what she wanted. She'd never lowered herself to blackmail before, but desperate times call for desperate measures. Leaning back in the recliner, Britney began speaking in an offhanded way, like what she was saying was of no consequence. "You know what I've been thinking about lately?"

"I'm sure you're going to tell me." Judge Hartman rolled her eyes, already bored with the conversation.

"I've been thinking about bearing my soul to this reporter who keeps calling asking for my story. He told me that he knows that I was pregnant by the senator and wants me to corroborate the story before he prints it."

The judge sat up, her hands clenched the edge of the desk.

"But I don't think the reporter should only write half of my story. So I was thinking about telling him about this house of horrors. Maybe unburden my soul by telling him how you let your perv of a husband rape me until Uncle Tony put a stop to it." Putting the recliner back in the upright position, Britney turned to her mother and asked, "I think that's a story that should be told, don't you?"

"I am sick to death of hearing about your precious Uncle Tony." When she said the word "uncle" her fingers made quotation marks in the air.

"Why do you do that whenever you get mad?" Britney imitated the quotation marks that her mother had just made concerning her uncle.

"Are we done with this conversation?" Judge Hartman asked.

"I guess we are. I have to catch up with that reporter anyway."

Shooting daggers at her daughter, Judge Hartman picked up the phone and dialed the chief of police. When he got on the phone, her voice didn't display any of the venom she was sending Britney's way. "Gilbert, how are you? I hear that congratulations are in order on that new grandbaby... You'll be receiving a big pink teddy bear for that precious baby girl... Look, I don't want to keep you. But for some reason your detectives have detained Bishop RaShawn Thomas and I've got to tell you, they have the wrong man. When the press gets wind of how your cops are wasting time on a dead end while a lunatic roams the streets free to kill again, I don't think this is going to look good for you... I think you're making the right decision. I would have released him too. Well, talk to you soon."

Britney stood as her mother hung up the phone. Judge Hartman told her, "Don't just stand there. You can at least thank me."

Instead of doing as her mother suggested, Britney strolled to the door. But just before leaving the room, she turned and said, "Oh, and just so you know... I won't be helping with anymore campaigns. I don't even want you to mention my name. Or like I said before, I just may get the itch to bear my soul."

***

"You and I have been sitting in this room for hours and lives are at stake. Tell me what you want so that I can get out of here and figure out a way to keep Marson and Williams alive."

"I don't think they want you anywhere near them," Detective Harris said.

"So what do you think happened here... what was my motive for killing these men?"

"Maybe you detest sin..."

"I do."

Harris continued, "...so much that you can't stand the fact that preachers would be wretched sinners themselves."

"My Bible tells me that all have sinned and come short of the glory of God, Detective."

Harris stood up and walked around the small room with his arms folded around his chest. "I read the Good Book too, Bishop. And do you know what has bothered me about you during this investigation?"

RaShawn looked up, following the detective's movements as he waited for him to continue. "In the 31st chapter of Jeremiah, verse 3 says: *The Lord has appeared of old to me saying, 'Yes, I have loved you with an everlasting love; therefore with loving kindness I have drawn you. Again I will build you, and you shall be rebuilt.'*"

"The thing is," Harris added as he sat back down with RaShawn, "I didn't see much love, kindness or rebuilding in what you did to those pastors. It seems as if you became bishop one day and then threw those pastors out of ministries they spent years building the next. So, if you could be that heartless, why do you find it so hard to believe that some of the officers in this building have pegged you for a killer?"

Had he been heartless? RaShawn hadn't seen it that way. He had been called to be God's battle axe. With that kind of calling, didn't it stand to reason that heads would roll? But never in a million years had RaShawn ever thought that following such a mandate from God would lead to this kind of destruction.

With death and destruction all around him, RaShawn had no defense for himself. Maybe he had been over zealous… maybe being God's battle axe didn't require him to chop down the tree just to get to the fruit. It was now clear to him that he owed Marson and Williams an apology for the way he'd handled things. So, yeah, he might be guilty of not dealing with the preachers in his fellowship with grace and loving kindness, but that was it. He looked Detective Harris in the eye and said, "I did not kill those men."

Getting comfortable in his seat, Harris told him, "I'm not your problem, Bishop. You see, I kind of believe that you're innocent of murder. But you've got to give me something to convince my boss that we're all wrong about this."

***

Governor Marcus and Raven Allen were seated in Captain McCoy's office reading him the riot act. "Has everyone in this godforsaken city gone mad? My brother-in-law is the most upstanding, honorable man I've ever had the pleasure to know. If it weren't for him, you all wouldn't have half the information about these murders."

"That's our problem, Governor. Bishop Thomas is too close to the situation. We wouldn't be doing our job if we didn't thoroughly check him out."

"Don't you get it?" Raven was practically screaming. "You're not doing your job at all. You are wasting time, while putting lives in jeopardy because the real killer is still out there."

"I want my brother-in-law out of that interrogation room this instant. I'm not playing games with you, McCoy. I may be the governor of Virginia, but you'll soon discover just how much power I have in D.C. if you allow this travesty to continue."

Chapter Nine

"You must have friends in high places, Bishop. The chief says we have to let you go."

He did indeed have one very special friend in the highest place. His name was Jesus and RaShawn trusted Him with his life. And now he was putting his faith in the Lord to help him make things right with the two pastors who were still alive.

Standing up, RaShawn asked, "Do you have someone watching out for Marson and Williams?"

"I sure do. So I suggest you keep your distance, because if you show up at another murder scene, even the chief of police won't be able to keep me from putting the cuffs on you."

"Something you said has convicted my spirit, Detective. I can guarantee you that I won't be at another murder scene, but I do need to speak with Daniel Marson and Marvel Williams."

"I just told you to stay away from them. Are you just itching to see what the inside of a prison cell looks like or what?"

"No, I'm not. But I need to make amends. There's no one that truly believes that I killed those men."

Detective Harris' left brow lifted. He opened his mouth to say something, but

RaShawn held up a hand. "All I'm asking is that you let me in to see these men. Either you or the officer guarding them can be present, but I have to see them."

Folding his arms around his chest, Jarod Harris asked, "Why is this so important to you?"

"Because you were right. I didn't handle any of these men with the loving kindness that God has dealt to all of us, nor did I even consider helping them to rebuild their lives. I abandoned them… basically left them for dead." With sadness clinging to his voice RaShawn said, "That's not who I am, Detective. Not who I am at all."

Harris unfolded his arms. He stared at RaShawn for a moment and then said, "Let me clear it with my captain and then I'll take you over there myself." Detective Harris opened the door and escorted him to a waiting area.

Marcus, Raven and Britney were there waiting for him. "You two got here fast. I guess you were the friends in high places Detective Harris was talking about," RaShawn said to his sister and brother-in-law.

Raven jumped up and hugged her brother. "I was so worried about you. And don't be mad at me, but Mama-Carmella and Daddy are on their way here."

"I'm not upset with you. After the day I've had, I'm thankful to see friendly faces," he assured her.

Marcus shook his hand and then said, "I don't think we were quite high enough to get you out of this jam. Raven and I were still arguing with the captain when the chief called in and told him to release you immediately." Marcus pointed in Britney's direction. "I think little Ms. Britney had something to do with that."

Britney stood, she walked slowly, but as she reached him, she couldn't help herself. She threw her arms around him and burst into tears.

RaShawn lifted her head with his index finger. He then proceeded to wipe the tears from her face. "Stop all that. All I was doing was sitting in a room talking to the detective."

"But they think you killed Linden."

"And you and I know that I didn't." He hugged her and then stepped back. "Have faith. God will take care of this."

Raven nudged her husband as she pointedly looked from RaShawn to Britney. She then whispered in his ear, "Told ya."

"Told him what?" RaShawn asked as he turned to his sister.

Raven started stuttering. "I…I."

Detective Harris walked over to them and saved her from having to say anything further. "Okay, the captain has given his approval. But there will have to be two officers present for your little meet and greet."

RaShawn handed Raven the keys to his house. "Can you all wait for me at the house? I can explain everything once I'm done."

"Where are you going?" Raven asked.

"I need to speak with Pastor Marson and Pastor Williams." That was the first time he'd called either of them pastor since he'd asked them to step down. He didn't know what that meant; either his heart was softening

74

towards them or the Lord was trying to lead him somewhere.

"I'll go with you," Britney said.

Detective Harris shook his head. "Just the Bishop or no go."

Detective Harris drove him to Daniel Marson's home first. During the drive, RaShawn just kept praying that God would give him wisdom. Which he had neglected to ask for when he'd taken on this position. But just as King Solomon had the good sense to realize he'd never be able to lead God's people without God's wisdom, so too, RaShawn should have realized the same thing. "Oh Lord, please forgive my folly and help me. Show me what being a battle axe for God truly means... lead me and I will follow."

As RaShawn lifted his head after praying, Detective Harris said, "I have often wondered how people know if they are truly following the Lord or their own selfish desires."

"When I figure it out, I'll let you know," RaShawn promised as they got out of the car.

Harris tapped on the police car at the curb. The officer got out of the car and followed them to the door.

When Marson opened the door his eyes flashed with surprise. "Didn't expect to see you at my door, Bishop." He opened the door wide. "Come on in."

"I would like to talk to you, if you don't mind," RaShawn said. There was a pleading sound to his voice.

Looking at him, Daniel Marson's brow arched as he asked, "What's this all about? I mean, I'm surprised that you want to talk to me now. Because the day you came to the church and asked me to step down, you didn't seem in the mood to hear anything I had to say."

"I was wrong for that."

Marson nodded, then pointed toward the sofa and a pair of chairs in his living room. He looked at the officers and asked jokingly, "Are you two here to make sure that the bishop doesn't kill me or something?"

"It's our job to ensure your safety, so we're just sitting in, but the two of you can go on as if we're not even here." Harris and the other officer sat down and kept quiet.

Marson turned back to RaShawn. "I'm listening."

Sitting down, RaShawn told him. "I'm here because someone helped me to realize that the way I handled things when I asked the six of you to step down, might have been a bit heavy handed... especially in your case."

"Why especially my case? Do you mean the fact that I wasn't sleeping with my members or stealing church funds? Is that what has softened your heart towards me?"

RaShawn could understand if Marson despised him for a lifetime. He had dismissed this man not because of sinful flaws, as the other preachers had been dismissed, but because he simply couldn't run an effective ministry if his life depended on it. "I may have been too harsh the last time we spoke. Maybe I should have partnered you with another pastor, someone who could have built you up in the skills that you lack."

Marson turned to the officers in the room. "Is this one of the worst apologies you've ever heard or what?"

Harris and the other officer laughed. "It is pretty bad."

Come on, Lord Jesus, I need You. "I don't mean to offend you," RaShawn said quickly. "I just believe that I could have handled your situation differently. And if I had,

76

you wouldn't be sitting here waiting to see if some maniac is going to try to kill you."

"I will admit that part is a problem for me," Marson said good naturedly. "That's probably the only bad thing about this situation."

"What do you mean?" RaShawn asked, confused by the fact that Marson didn't consider losing his ministry to be a bad thing.

"Don't get me wrong," Marson said, "I was very angry with you when you asked me to step down. Johnson, Brown and Hartman," he counted off the pastors who had been fired before him, "I understood why you asked them to step down, because everyone knew how raggedy their lives were. But I hadn't done any of those things, so I kept telling myself that there had been some kind of mistake.

"But God doesn't make mistakes. So, then I started praying and asking Him what He wanted from me. And do you know what I discovered?"

RaShawn shook his head.

"I discovered that although I loved the people in the ministry, I dreaded just about everything else about leading a ministry. God showed me that I am an evangelist. So, now I'm just waiting on Him to send me wherever there is a need."

RaShawn felt the Lord nudging him, bringing back to his remembrance the fact that he needed an evangelist for the revival this weekend. "I don't know how you feel about hanging out with me, but I believe that the Lord has opened a spot for you. I happen to be in need of an evangelist for this weekend's revival."

Marson steepled his hands as he closed his eyes and said a quick prayer. When he opened his eyes again, he smiled at RaShawn. "I'm in. That is, if my police detail will allow me to preach at the event."

"Just don't drink any grape juice," Detective Harris said.

"That reminds me. I think I need to cancel the communion for this Sunday. We use the pre-made communion cups, but just to be on the safe side, I don't think we'll be passing that out until you catch this Avenger person."

After leaving Marson's home, Detective Harris and RaShawn drove over to Marvel Williams' house. But things did not go as well with Marvel. There would be no reconciliation. RaShawn hadn't even been able to apologize to Marvel about the harsh way in which he'd spoken to the man at their last meeting.

Marvel opened his front door and the moment he saw RaShawn, he shouted, "Get off my porch."

"If you can just give me a few minutes, Marvel. I just want to speak with you about our last meeting."

"You and I have said everything we're ever going to say to each other. I tried to tell you that I need to support my son, but you wouldn't listen."

"I may have been a bit harsh when speaking with you that day, and I wish I could have been more respectful in the way I spoke to you, but even though I still don't agree with what you did. I'm ready to listen."

Marvel's lip curled, he almost cursed RaShawn, but instead decided to slam the door in his face.

RaShawn lifted his hand to knock on the door, but Detective Harris stopped him. "Count your blessings, Bishop. At least Marson isn't still holding a grudge. You really didn't expect both of them to sing songs of praise with you tonight, did you?"

"That would have been nice," RaShawn admitted as he stepped off Marvel's porch with his head held low.

"Cheer up, Bishop, 50/50 ain't bad," Harris told him as they got into his car.

This wasn't a popularity contest. God didn't call him to make friends. So RaShawn should have worn the fact that Marvel Williams couldn't stand the sight of him like a badge of honor. After all, Marvel was the one who stood in his pulpit and married his son to another man, as if God would ever be okay with that.

The fact that Marvel Williams couldn't just admit that he was wrong and repent, was astonishing to RaShawn. He had to find a way to show Marvel the truth of God.

Chapter Ten

Britney was going to get answers about her mother's weird behavior concerning Uncle Tony. Since her father and uncle were both deceased, she turned to the only person she'd be able to get the truth from.

Aunt Carla had been married to her uncle for thirty years before she finally divorced him. She loved him and tried to stay with him. But her uncle didn't know how to treat the woman he'd told her on many occasions was the love of his life. Now he was dead and Auntie Carla was the only one she could turn to.

They clung to each other as any two people would who'd experienced a loss that cut deep down into their souls. "How are you doing, honey?" Carla asked as they broke apart.

"I've been better, but I don't have to tell you that."

"You certainly don't." Carla put an arm around Britney and went into the family room with her. As they sat down across from each other, Carla smiled at her as she asked, "So what brings you all this way out here?"

"I can hardly believe that you're living on a farm now. You always seemed like such a city girl to me." Britney needed a moment. She didn't know how to just come out and ask her question, so talking about the farm beat talking about the weather.

"I never thought I'd like being more than twenty miles from the nearest mall either. But it's so serene and peaceful out here… this place turned out to be just what I needed."

"I wish you and Uncle Tony had this place when I was a kid. I would have loved feeding chickens and being able to ride a horse in all this space you have out here."

"I wish you and my other kids could have enjoyed the peacefulness of this place when you were kids too. But Tony didn't like country living. Everything had to be fast-paced for that husband of mine."

Britney smiled as she remembered the corvette and the mustang her uncle kept in his garage and constantly tinkered with. But then she backtracked, as something that Carla said took on a deeper meaning than it ever had the numerous times she'd heard her say it before. "You've always included me when you speak of your children, and I spent every summer with you and most holidays too. Why would you and Uncle Tony do all that for me when you didn't have to?"

Putting a hand on Britney's arm, Carla said, "Because we love you, sweetheart."

"I know you love me. And I'm so thankful for that. I felt so unloved at home, but every time I stayed with you and Uncle Tony, I felt as if I was part of a real family, you know?"

Carla nodded. "We prayed that you would feel that way when you were with us."

Getting to the reason for her visit, Britney said, "I'm just confused about a few things and I was hoping that you could help me understand some things."

"Are you hungry?" Carla asked popping up. "I was just about to fix some dinner when you arrived."

Britney grabbed hold of her aunt's hand. "Do you mind if we eat later? I really need to talk to you."

Carla sat back down, fear etched across her face as she said, "Okay, ask away."

"I never knew my father. According to my mom, he died two weeks before I was born in a car accident. The marriage certificate shows that they were only married for three months. And I pulled my birth certificate and no father was listed. Why wouldn't she have listed Philip Hartman as my father if he really was? It shouldn't have mattered that he died; she was his wife, so the hospital would have allowed his name to go on my birth certificate, right?"

"She was supposed to put Phillip's name on your birth certificate, but after he died, your mother refused to do it."

"Why?" Britney asked, not understanding any of the strangeness that went on in her family.

Closing her eyes, Carla took a deep breath and then spoke the truth. "Because Philip wasn't your real father."

Britney wanted to be surprised, shocked, appalled even. But her mother had done so much to her that the knowledge that she had lied about who her father was did nothing more than cause an *aha* moment. "That's why she always acts as if Tony is only my "play" uncle when she gets mad at him. She knew that he was only pretending to be my uncle because she had tricked his poor unsuspecting brother into marrying her."

"There's more to it than that, I'm afraid."

Britney's eyebrow arched as she stared at her "aunt." "How can there be more than this? Don't tell me that my real father was some serial killer... or a drug addict. But actually, I would believe it if he were a drug addict... that would explain why I had been drawn to drugs so easily."

"Tony came to see me about two weeks before he died. He told me that he couldn't live with so many secrets anymore. He wanted to tell you everything. I agreed with him, so I guess the task has been left to me now."

"I was supposed to have breakfast with him the same week he died." Putting her hands over her face, she admitted, "I would have been so sad if he had told me that he isn't actually my uncle."

"Tony loved you so dearly. I believe he loved me too. But what you have to understand is that he didn't love either of us more than he loved himself... he wasn't prepared to sacrifice his ministry for you and he wouldn't stop his womanizing so that we could be happy."

"What are you saying? Why would Uncle Tony need to sacrifice his ministry for me?" Britney was getting this awful feeling in the pit of her stomach.

"At the end, though, he was a changed man. Bishop Thomas asking him to step down had humbled him... made him look over the lives he'd destroyed along the way. He made amends with me and our kids and he wanted to do the same with you."

Tears rolled down Britney's face as she waited for her aunt to say the words that would forever change the dynamic of her belief system. Tony had always been a hero to her, but was her aunt now telling her that he was actually nothing more than a man who willfully neglected his responsibilities?

"Tony was your father."

The fact that her mother had lied to her all these years had been nothing new, and hadn't upset Britney in the least. But to know that her beloved uncle was actually her father and that he left her in that house of horrors with only summer and holiday breaks was more than she could digest.

Her chest heaved as a rain forest of tears covered her face. Britney wrapped a hand around her mouth and ran to the bathroom. She prostrated herself in front of the toilet. Carla ran up behind her and pulled back her hair as Britney heaved and released... heaved and released until the contents of her stomach had emptied.

Carla handed her a towel to wipe her mouth. "It's okay, hon. You have a right to be upset. But don't you ever forget how much Tony and I loved you."

"Why didn't anyone tell me? Why did he leave me with those awful people?" Sitting down on the bathroom floor, Britney tried to make sense out of everything she now knew.

"I don't expect you to understand, 'cause it was complicated. Your mother thought that Tony would marry her once she told him she was pregnant. When he offered up his brother instead, she never forgave him. We rarely saw you the first few years of your life. But when Lisa became a judge, she finally relented. She had worked so hard to get that position, she didn't want a scandal of any kind."

Anger boiled up in Britney. She got off the floor and dried her eyes. "You know what, Aunt Carla, I think it's high time that my mother gets what's coming to her. She has always treated me like I was the worst thing that ever happened to her and now I know why."

"What are you going to do?"

"I'm going to introduce the world to the real Lisa Hartman."

"Be careful, honey, your mother doesn't fight fair."

"Neither do I," Britney said as she grabbed her purse and headed back to the city.

***

The revival kicked off in the morning and RaShawn still wasn't settled in his spirit. Marvel Williams was heavy on his mind. He feared that the way he'd handled the situation with Marvel might have caused the man to turn away from God and ministry altogether. He couldn't allow that to happen, not when Marvel's soul was in jeopardy.

Daniel Marson and Marvel Williams had always been tight and had supported each other in ministry through the years. A thought struck RaShawn and he picked up the phone. "I hope this is coming from You, Lord, 'cause I'm fresh out of ideas." He dialed Marson's number and waited until it was picked up. "Hey, Minister Marson, I don't want to keep you; I'm sure you're putting your sermon together for tomorrow, but I need a favor."

"What kind favor?" Marson asked.

"I'd like you to invite Marvel to the revival. I truly believe that God wants him to be there."

"Will he be able to sit in the pulpit with us?"

The man hadn't repent for using God's pulpit for an ungodly purpose yet. RaShawn strongly believed any man or woman seated behind a pulpit is a representative of God. And at the very least, he or she should believe the words written in the Bible. "No, not yet. I just wanted you to ask him to come and support your new calling."

After a brief silence Marson said, "I can do that."

After hanging up with Marson, RaShawn remembered that he needed to tell Britney something. He called her cell, but didn't get an answer... left her a message to call and then headed back into the family room to talk with his family. They were spending the night so they could attend the revival with him.

"Why the long face?" Raven asked as RaShawn sat down with them.

"I was just thinking about Marvel Williams. I don't think I handled the situation in love, the way I believe God would have wanted it handled."

"Are you having second thoughts about firing him?" Carmella asked, putting her book on the coffee table.

"What are you reading?" RaShawn asked, picking up the book.

"A book about the difference between today's Christians and the Christians in Roman times. The author makes some good points."

RaShawn was intrigued. "Do you mind if I take a look at it?"

"Have at it," Carmella told him.

"Thanks, and no, I don't regret letting him go. But I do regret how harshly I spoke to him. I think I missed something that might determine whether he totally walks away from God or rediscovers his place."

"You're being too hard on yourself, son. Remember, you were not even in your new position a day when you'd been asked to clean up all the mess those pastors had left behind," Ramsey reminded him.

"That is true," RaShawn acknowledged. "But I can't help feeling that I missed something where Marvel was concerned. The man had once been on fire for the Lord. I just don't know what happened to him."

"There's no sense beating yourself up about it," Carmella said as she stood up and held out her hands. "Let's go to God and ask Him to reveal everything He needs you to know about Marvel."

RaShawn thought about the dream he had, where Marvel had reached out to him for help, but RaShawn had been lost... he hadn't known what kind of help he could give a man like Marvel, someone who had tried to turn the truth of God into a lie. "Sounds like a plan to me." RaShawn grabbed hold of Carmella's hand as his dad, Raven and Marcus joined them.

Chapter Eleven

Britney ignored RaShawn's call as she drove back into town. Her heart was bleeding from the inside out and she didn't think she would be able to talk to him without bursting into tears. RaShawn had enough going on. He didn't need her burdening him with her problems.

For a brief moment Britney thought about calling some of the friends she used to hang out with when she'd needed to numb her mind to the pain her mother had caused during her childhood. But the thought of that terrified her, so she started praying like the devil himself was chasing her, trying to get her to turn back. There was no way she would ever go back to what she had been... not as long as there was still breath in her body and she could call out for help from her Lord and Savior Jesus Christ.

After praying, Britney felt as if she had reined her emotions in enough to talk to RaShawn, so she picked up her cell and called him. He answered on the second ring.

"Hey, you. Where've you been all day?"

"I was visiting with Carla."

"I'm sure she appreciated the company," RaShawn said.

His voice sounded so soothing, so comforting that Britney almost told him right then and there about Tony being her father. But she held back, the wound was too fresh, she needed distance from the pain before she could talk about this with RaShawn. "She was happy to see me," was all she said in response.

"I hope that you'll be at the revival tomorrow. I'd love to look out and see that beautiful smile of yours."

He was always saying such nice things to her... treating her as if he knew nothing of her past. RaShawn was truly something special; she thanked God every day for sending him her way. He showed her what true Christianity looked like. After growing up with her mother's brand of Christianity, Britney had wanted nothing to do with the faith. But she no longer blamed God for the fakes who pretended to bow down before Him, while in truth they only served themselves and did what was right in their own eyes. "Of course I will be there. I wouldn't miss it for the world. I'll talk to you later; I just pulled up at my mom's house."

"Before you hang up, I called you for a reason."

"Oh yeah, right." She got so distracted when talking to this man. Hopefully, God could reveal something about that to her. Either move this thing to the next level, or help her to move on.

"I just realized why Marson was skipped over and Linden was killed instead."

"Huh?"

"Remember? You had thought that the killer was taking each preacher out based on when I had asked them to step down. But when Linden was killed before Marson, we basically ditched that theory."

"Gotcha. So what do you think happened? Maybe the killer had his timeline wrong?"

"Not at all. I think the killer knows exactly what he's doing. And if my theory is correct, then Marson has never been a target."

"And why is that?"

"Because Marson wasn't fired because he was caught doing some ungodly act. I let him go because he was totally disorganized and disinterested in being in the office of a pastor. Marson is an evangelist and he's happy to take on that role."

"And the killer knew that... so our other assumption has to be correct as well. Whoever is killing these pastors has to be a member of the board."

"I'm going to call Senior Bishop Brown and Detective Harris and tell them what we've figured out. Hopefully, the two of them can work together to figure out who has taken it upon themselves to be judge, jury and sentencer."

"You do that. I need to take care of something over here. But I'll see you tomorrow." They hung up then Britney took a deep breath as she prepared herself to deal with the enemy within.

The queen bee was waiting for her. Apparently Carla had called. Britney didn't know who she was angrier at, her mother the deceiver or Carla the peacemaker. She folded her arms as she stood in front of the massive desk her mother seemed to spend a lifetime behind.

"I know you're upset, Britney, but I hope that you are laying blame where it's deserved."

"You're not even going to deny any of this?"

She lifted her hands. "Why should I? I held up my end of the bargain. I pretended that another man was your father all these years. But when I wanted my secret protected, he didn't care about that. And neither did your precious little Aunt Carla."

"You leave her out of this. Carla has been better to me than you ever were on your best day. So, don't disparage her."

Rising from her seat like a pit bull spotting its prey, Judge Hartman said, "You better hope disparaging her is all I do. I'm of a mind to go over there and break her neck."

Backing up as fear crept up her spine at the hate she saw in her mother's eyes, she asked, "Why are you so evil? All these years you've pretended to be a Christian to the outside world. But at home, I never witnessed anything Christ-like about you."

"Now who's disparaging whom?" Stepping around her desk and coming towards her daughter, Lisa said, "I did everything a mother could do for you. I made sure you were clothed, fed, I put you in the right schools but you didn't appreciate any of it. All you ever did was throw your Uncle Tony and his precious wife in my face. Do you know how many times I wanted to tell you to your face that Tony didn't love you? He never even wanted you."

"He loved me. He was going to tell me the truth. He called and asked me to come see him. If he hadn't died, he would have tried to make this right... I know he would have."

Lisa laughed in her daughter's face. "Are you really that dumb? How could he make anything right after ignoring the truth for this long?"

"Why do you hate him so much?" Britney asked. She wondered for so long, but never had the guts to demand an answer. But now, in light of everything that she now knew to be true, the least her mother could do was fill in the blanks.

"For the same reason that you should hate him. After his brother died in that car accident, Tony being the wonderful man he was, couldn't bear that I should have to raise you alone. So, he provided another husband for me."

Britney's eyes grew wide.

"That's right," Lisa continued. "Your stepfather had been a member of Tony's church. Back in those days I was so green, I didn't know how to do anything but trust. And Tony knew I would marry him on the spot, because he was a judge and had connections that got me my first seat behind the bench."

Looking far off, as if seeing some distant memory, Lisa continued, "I still remember the day Tony discovered that he'd married me off to a pedophile. He begged me to divorce him, but I refused. By that time I hated my husband, but I hated Tony more."

Britney felt as if she was going to be sick again. But she refused to give her mother the satisfaction. "You obviously hated me too. Or you would have put a stop to what your husband was doing long before Uncle Tony stopped him."

Sounding as if she was the victim, Lisa said, "You have no idea what it was like for me back then."

"I think it's time to stop all the secrecy. I'm tired of it. And I have decided that I am going to meet with that reporter and unload on him. I hope to God that what I have to say destroys your career. Since that's the only thing you seem to care about."

"Careful, Britney, Tony didn't fare too well after attempting to expose me. I would hate for the same thing to happen to you."

"Are you threatening me?" Then Britney did a rewind as she realized the implications of what her mother had just said. "Did you have something to do with Uncle Tony's death?"

"Don't be absurd. Look, sit down and let's talk this out before you do something you'll regret." Lisa reached out a hand and wrapped it around Britney's arm.

As her mom extended her hand, Britney noticed something in between her fingers. She tried to move out of her reach, but wasn't quick enough. She felt a prick as if a needle had penetrated her flesh and then turned an accusing eye toward her mother.

"Oh, don't look at me as if I betrayed you. Things will be better this way, you'll see."

"What did you do to me?" Realizing that she needed to get away, Britney didn't wait for an answer. She unraveled her mother's fingers from her arm and bolted for the door... only, it didn't feel as if she was running very fast. Felt more like slogging through quicksand. She grabbed hold of the doorknob and was about to open it when her whole body went limp and she fell face first on the floor.

***

Meanwhile, Rita was in her prayer closet communing with the Lord. He had brought her a long way. These days when she looked in the mirror she still saw the beauty queen that was able to catch the eye of just about any man she desired. But that no longer mattered to her. She was no longer ready and willing to sell her soul to the highest bidder. She paid her own rent and took care of her child. Life was good.

The only problem she had was Britney's thrill-seeking behavior. She worried about that girl and now it seemed as if she was getting another premonition about something bad happening to her friend. "Lord, please tell me what's going on; I feel as if Britney needs me. But I don't know what to do."

Find her.

Rita heard the response and didn't waste time asking again. She finished her prayer and then ran to the telephone. Britney wasn't answering the phone so she left two messages. She sat down and waited twenty minutes for her friend to call back.

Britney thought she worried too much. But Rita trusted the Lord, and if He was nudging her too, then there must be a reason for that. "Right?" she said to Tyler as she pulled her out of her baby bed, put her shoes on and headed out the door.

Chapter Twelve

"No... no! Stay away from me!" Seven-year-old Britney ran to the other side of her bedroom and huddled in the corner. Her mommy was out of town, and Britney had begged her not to leave because she knew what would happen the moment the lights went out in this horrible house.

He smelled of booze as he approached her, slurring his words. *"Don't make me chase after you."*

"Leave me alone," she shouted.

But he grabbed hold of her arm and pulled her out towards the door. *"You've been bad today. You have to learn how to be a good little girl."*

"I'll be good. I promise. Just leave me alone," Britney begged as tears ran down her face.

"I told you before, if you do right, I won't do wrong. Now get in here and let me teach you how to be a good little girl."

Panting as if her heart was about to pound its way out of her chest, Britney bolted upright. Terror stricken, she searched her surroundings. Realizing that she wasn't seven years old anymore and that she was having a nightmare, her breathing slowly normalized. "Where am I?" The room was pitch black.

Charles had said those words to her... but Charles was dead.

Standing up, she searched around for a light switch, but couldn't find one. Then she felt her eyes drooping as her knees buckled and she was once again stretched out on the floor. She was sinking back to a place she didn't want to be. She wasn't seven years old anymore. She was now fourteen and things had changed in the house. Her mother had just won her first elected post as a judge and thanks to her Uncle Tony, her stepfather hadn't abused her in the last two years.

Her mother walked the halls, carrying a silver tray containing red wine, crackers and two wine glasses. She took the tray into her bedroom and left the door open as she set it down on the nightstand.

Britney prayed that her mother wasn't about to give that wine to her stepfather. She knew firsthand what he was like when he was drunk. Tiptoeing into the hallway, Britney made her way to her mother's bedroom door. She stood watching. Her mother had told her that her stepfather had some kind of flu bug which had caused him to be bedridden for the past week.

Britney had been thrilled when he'd taken to his bed and hadn't been able to roam the halls. But she feared that alcohol might make him better and then he'd once again be in her face, telling her to 'do right, so he wouldn't have to do wrong.'

Lisa said, "Wake up, Charles. You and I need to talk."

"Wha... where am I?" he asked, as if he didn't even know that he was in his own bed.

"It's me, Charles... Lisa. Now wake up. You don't have much time left."

"Why do I feel so terrible?" he asked, barely able to lift himself up.

She didn't answer that, but said, "You've outlived your usefulness to me, Charles. You won't survive much longer. I know you feel your body weakening."

"What have you done to me?"

"Let me help you sit up." She adjusted the pillows behind him and then lifted him to an upright position. Lisa then put the communion tray on the bed next to him as she asked, "Don't you think you should repent before it's too late?"

Struggling to breathe, Charles asked, "Am I dying?"

She nodded. "Yes, Charles, you are."

His head fell back against his pillow, as he cried out to God. "Please forgive me for my sins... for my weakness."

"That's good, Charles. You don't have to say anymore. Hold your strength so you can take communion. Remember how you told me that communion cleanses all of our sins?"

He nodded, tears running down his face.

"Take the cracker." She handed him the cracker and said, "This is the body of Jesus, which was broken for you... even for a vile sinner like you."

Charles quickly ate the cracker.

She ate hers and then poured wine in both their glasses. Before handing Charles his glass, Britney saw her mom open a small vile and pour something into his wine.

Her stepfather drank the wine, laid down the glass, said, "I'm sorry" to Lisa and then laid his head back against the pillow.

Britney kept staring at him, waiting for him to move again, but he never did. Her mother got off the bed and looked directly at her. "Oh Britney, dear, I didn't know you were there. I'm afraid your stepfather has passed away. I need to call the undertaker so he can be cremated as he always wanted."

***

RaShawn was ready. After staying up all night studying Roman history, he had finally managed to prepare his sermon. The first two days of the revival would be televised. RaShawn only prayed that God's people tuned in and that they opened their ears as well as their hearts. But once again, he had Carmella Marshall-Thomas to thank. Because if she hadn't come to town and brought her book on Roman times with her, RaShawn wouldn't have made the connection as far as what God wanted from him.

When he walked into the kitchen, all he was thinking about was grabbing a quick breakfast before leaving for the revival. But Rita and her little girl were seated at the table. She had a disturbed look on her face as she talk with Raven and Marcus.

"I didn't know that you were coming to town for the revival," RaShawn said as he took Tyler out of her arms.

"I hadn't plan to be here. But I have to find Britney," Rita told him.

Bouncing the baby in his arms, RaShawn said, "She'll be at the revival, so you'll see her there if you come with us."

Rita stood up. "Here's the thing. I don't see her at the revival. I see her lying on the floor of a dark room that doesn't get sunlight."

"She had one of her premonitions," Raven told RaShawn.

RaShawn handed the baby back to Rita. "I've got to go get her."

"Hold on," Marcus stood. "You have a revival to get to. We were just trying to figure out where Britney might have gotten off to, so I can go get her."

Like the wind was being knocked out of him, RaShawn pushed the words out, "When she called me last night... she told me that she had just pulled up to her mother's house."

"I know where Judge Hartman lives," Marcus told RaShawn. "You go on to the revival. And I'll go check on Britney."

"I'm coming with you," Raven said. "You'll need an extra pair of hands if Judge Hartman and Britney are laid out in that house."

"Wait, Britney wouldn't have spent the night at her mother's. She told me that house gives her the creeps." Rita said.

RaShawn then told Marcus and Raven the name and address of the hotel Britney had checked into. "Ask the hotel clerk to let you into her room."

As Marcus and Raven left Rita turned to RaShawn. "Can we ride to the revival with you? I can look around the church to see if Britney shows up."

"Sounds like a plan," RaShawn said as they all left the house.

***

Judge Hartman knocked on the cellar door. She waited a moment then knocked again. "Wake up, Britney."

"Go away."

"Don't be like that, Britney. I've tried everything I can think of to help you. I don't know why you keep going back to drugs."

"What are you talking about? I'm not on drugs." But as she said those words she heard the slur in her voice, and then recognized the sleepy feeling that seemed to overtake her senses. She'd been nodding off in this room and being forced to deal with her nightmares for hours now.

"I found your drugs and your needle, so there's no use in denying it. I called Dr. Sellers and he will be here to get you within the hour."

"You drugged me? How could you do that?" Britney tried to get up, but found herself stumbling backwards. She now knew her mother to be a cold-blooded murderer, but she'd never expected that she would actually put the very thing that Britney had struggled long and hard to get away from back into her system. "Lord Jesus, I need help. Please..." was all she could say before tears rolled down her face.

"Call on the Lord all you want. Just know that no reporter will believe a word you say now. Not when you can't even stay off of drugs."

Chapter Thirteen

RaShawn couldn't concentrate. He was scheduled to deliver his message in less than ten minutes, but still hadn't received word that Britney had been located. He walked over to Rita. "Have you heard anything?"

She shook her head. "But Judge Hartman just walked in." She pointed to the front of the church.

Just as Judge Hartman was about to take her seat, the senior bishop rushed over to her. As RaShawn watched them smile and chit-chat, the fact that Judge Hartman was on the board of their church fellowship crossed his mind. "Let's go talk to her."

RaShawn didn't have time to wait his turn, so he tapped the Bishop David Brown on the shoulder and asked if he could borrow the judge for a moment. She moved to the side of the church with Rita and RaShawn. Then RaShawn said, "We haven't been able to find Britney. I was hoping that you might know where she is."

Shaking her head, Judge Hartman told him, "I haven't seen Britney since the funeral. I thought she was with you or with Rita."

"We don't have time for your games, Judge Hartman," Rita said with the baby on one hip and her hand perched on the other. "We know Britney was at your house last night. Now you need to tell us where she is."

Looking as if she'd like to wring Rita's neck, she turned to RaShawn and said, "I was trying to keep this from you until after you delivered your message, but Britney is sick."

"What do you mean? What's wrong with her?"

Shrugging her shoulders and sighing deeply, Judge Hartman said, "She was whacked out of her mind on drugs when she came to my house last night. I called Dr. Sellers. He's picking her up now and taking her back to rehab."

That made absolutely no sense to RaShawn. Britney had conquered that beast. No way would she turn back like a dog licking his vomit. "I'm sorry to hear that. Thanks for telling us," he said as he took hold of Rita's arm and walked away from the judge.

"You don't honestly believe that, do you?" Rita was saying, but RaShawn shushed her.

He rushed Rita to the back of the church and said, "Call Raven and tell her to turn around and go to Judge Hartman's house. And tell Marcus use the full weight of his governorship to ensure that Dr. Sellers releases Britney."

"Okay," she said in a much calmer voice, now that she knew that Bishop Thomas didn't believe the judge. "You had better get to the pulpit, the senior bishop just looked at his watch, then glanced over here."

"I'm on my way. I just need to make one quick call," RaShawn said as he headed to his office.

***

"Listen to me, Dr. Sellers. I don't have a drug problem and my mother is evil. She kills people for fun." But as Britney thought about everything that happened, she realized that the killings didn't start until her father wanted to reveal himself to her. So maybe her mother wasn't some thrill-seeking kind of killer...maybe she only wanted to kill Uncle Tony, but to get away with it, she staged this whole Avenger of Sins thing.

She sat up straight with her hands extended. "No, wait. She doesn't like killing people. She just wanted to kill my uncle... I mean, my father, who I thought was my uncle."

Dr. Sellers glanced at the housekeeper who had let him in the house so that he could get Britney. "She's manic. I'm going to need you to help hold her down so I can give her a sedative."

Britney got up and ran behind the sofa. "I'm not manic, just listen to me, okay?"

Dr. Sellers opened his bag and pulled out a syringe. "We're just going to get you calmed down and then we can talk."

Britney turned frightened eyes toward the housekeeper. "I know you haven't worked here long, but you've got to believe me. My mom is a monster."

"She says you're a drug addict," the housekeeper said with a strong Jamaican accent.

"Grab her," Dr. Sellers yelled.

The housekeeper rushed her. Britney's reflexes were off because of what her mother had put into her system, so the housekeeper was able to tackle and get her on the floor with very little opposition. But as Britney turned pleading eyes on the woman and said, "Help me… please," she felt the woman's hold loosen, then the doorbell rang, and rang and rang. Then someone started beating on the door like Satan and all his imps was after him.

"This is Governor Marcus Allen."

The instant Britney heard his voice, she started thanking the Lord. Because she knew He had answered her plea for help.

"Open this door or I'll have the police here in a matter of minutes."

***

RaShawn stood in front of the podium with his Bible open, ready to do God's will; he now had a clearer understanding of what His will truly was. Yes, he was called to be God's battle axe. But RaShawn no longer thought that meant to tear down all the no-good preachers. Rather, God had him on a mission to root out sin. His mission was to chop sin down to the root and then dig it up and put it on display, so that the people who belonged to God could see clearly, and would then be able to find their way back home.

He said a silent prayer for Britney, trusting that God would take care of her. He opened his Bible, turned to Romans 12:2 and began reading: *"Do not be conformed to this world, but be transformed by the renewing of your mind, that you may prove what is that good and acceptable and perfect will of God."*

Looking out at the congregation he said, "Apostle Paul wrote those words during a time in Roman society when Christians were hated for their belief in moral purity. You see, when Rome was at the height of its glory and power, there existed a group of people who dared to challenge the immoral and wicked behavior that had become common.

"These Christians refused to be absorbed into the godless society of Rome. They'd never heard the saying, 'When in Rome, do as the Romans do.' Nor, were they among the 'live and let live' crowd. Therefore the Roman high tribunal decided to stamp out Christianity because they were considered disturbers of pagan unity."

His dad and Mama-Carmella were seated on the front row. RaShawn caught the smile that appeared on Mama-Carmella's face as she realized that he had indeed read the book he'd borrow from her last night. He smiled back at her as he continued. "The Romans had a false notion that they could control a person's conscience by implementing laws that made it illegal to be different. Everyone had to bow to Caesar... all had to conform to pagan customs or be threatened with death. In those days many Christians chose death rather than conform to Rome and compromise the faith they had in the only true God.

"I can hear you now, silently thanking God that you live in America, where all are free. But if we are so free, why are so many Christians conforming to the immorality of this era... saying that wrong is right and declaring, 'Who am I to judge?'

"Do you know why Christians are now afraid to quote the very Bible they are supposed to be reading," he held up his Bible, "and declare abortion, lust, fornication and homosexuality is sin? It is because they have been backed into a corner and fear that their livelihood will be taken away if they speak up for the truth of God.

"So, I tell you that the Christians of today are nothing like the Christians in Roman times. Those Christians would have loved for someone to just make it hard for them to earn a living, rather than feeding them to hungry lions.

"The Apostle Paul urges Christians to be nonconformists as far as the world system is concerned. Because a true Christian, living an obedient life is a constant rebuke to those who accept the moral standards of this world. Our Lord warned His disciples in John 15:18, 'If the world hates you, you know that it hated Me before it hated you.'"

Marvel Williams was seated about three rows behind his parents. Tears were streaming down the man's face. But the way he glared up at the pulpit, RaShawn knew that those were not tears of repentance, but of hot anger. But RaShawn would not be deterred from the mission he'd received from God.

Pounding on the podium he declared as it says in 2nd Timothy 3:12: "Do you not know that all who live godly in Christ Jesus will suffer persecution!"

"The word of God teaches that popularity with the world means death. Satan's most effective tools are conformity and compromise. He is aware that one man standing in the midst of a pagan nation declaring, 'I am not ashamed of the gospel of Christ, for it is the power of God to salvation for everyone who believes,' can move more sinners in the direction of God than thousands of weak, compromising Christians.

"The words of Apostle Paul, 'Do not be conformed to this world,' have a great deal of significance and meaning for us in this day and age. These words cut like a sharp sword to those of us who have allowed our family and friends or the things that entertain us, like movies and music, to cause us to conform. But Apostle Paul's words are like a battle cry… calling out to all who claim the name of Jesus Christ. His words separate the weak from the strong. They are words of inspiration, encouraging the believer to press on toward the prize of the high calling of Jesus Christ.

"Will you join me, saints? Will you stand up for the truth of God and not prostrate yourself before the temple of the Baal of this age? I challenge you to present yourself holy and acceptable to God… Let's be a living sacrifice and let the rest of the world stand back and witness the glory of God." As RaShawn closed the Bible and stepped away from the podium, the congregation went wild. They stood and gleefully applauded his message.

But RaShawn wasn't deceived by the applause. He was standing in front of like-minded people. But the conference was being televised… soon, the persecution would come.

Chapter Fourteen

Marvel Williams had been ready to leave two minutes into RaShawn's sermon, but he didn't want to bring attention to himself. So, he stayed in his seat, fuming over the message. Who was he to judge him? Bishop Thomas knew nothing of him or what his family suffered because of Marvel's commitment to Christ.

He had planned to stick around to support Daniel. The choir would sing and the offering would be taken before his friend stood behind the podium. But Marvel didn't think he could sit there and pretend that he was just fine with the message that had just been preached, when in truth, he was livid. Now that others were up milling around, Marvel didn't want to miss his opportunity to quietly leave the building.

He had reached the fellowship hall and was almost at the door when Judge Hartman stopped him. "Hey, Pastor Williams, where are you rushing off to?"

Marvel shook his head. "I've got to get out of here."

"But your friend is about to preach, don't you want to stick around and support him?"

"If I stay here any longer, I just might explode. Excuse me, Judge Hartman, but I need to leave."

As he stepped past her, Judge Hartman lightly touched his arm. She moved closer and said, "I wasn't in agreement with the rest of the board members when they voted to let you go. I thought the situation could have and should have been handled in a much more productive manner."

Marvel looked in Judge Hartman's eyes, as if he were searching for understanding. "I've always tried to do what was right. But I had to be there for my son."

"If it wasn't for the fact that the board had been looking for a fresh face to take over, you might have been the new bishop. Would you like to go into Bishop Thomas' office so we can discuss your future, and how I might be able to help you?"

Wouldn't it be something if after being fired from his pastoral position, he then became bishop and was able to make the changes he saw fit within this confining organization? Marvel liked the thought of that very much and quickly agreed to speak with her in Bishop Thomas' office... an office that, if things went right, could soon belong to him.

***

Marcus and Raven helped Britney along as they entered the church. The effects of the drugs that had been injected into her system were fading, but she still wasn't a hundred percent yet.

Rita ran over to them the moment they entered the sanctuary. "Thank God you're okay. I don't know what I would have done if something happened to you."

Britney pulled her best friend into her arms. "Thank God for those premonitions of yours. I promise I'll listen to you from now on."

"You better," Rita said as she wagged a finger in her face.

Before Britney could respond to that, she felt strong hands pulling her away from Rita. Turning, she saw RaShawn as he pulled her into his arms. "God is a prayer-answering God," he proclaimed, then said, "I was so worried about you. Are you okay?"

"I will be," she assured him.

"Where's Judge Hartman?" Marcus asked.

RaShawn pointed to the front of the church. "She was sitting over there with the other board members."

"I didn't know she was on the board for this fellowship," Britney said as all the pieces came together.

"She joined the board about two years before I came here," RaShawn told them.

"We can't let her leave this building, RaShawn; she's the killer."

RaShawn stepped back, looked at Britney. "Your mother? The judge... is a killer?"

"Yes." Britney nodded. "I think that my mother once believed in God and wanted to be a true Christian. But she has been messed over by one too many men claiming to be men of God. I think that's why she snapped."

"I don't understand." RaShawn still wasn't getting it. He didn't know how someone could go from being a judge, charged with upholding the law, to spree killing.

"I'll fill you in on everything later. But if we don't find her, she will not stop until she has finished Pastor Williams off."

RaShawn turned back to the sanctuary, searching for Marvel. "He was just here. I looked right at him while I was preaching." RaShawn turned this way and that, then finally rushed out of the sanctuary and into the fellowship hall, looking from one end of the room to the next, but Marvel was not in there either. He went outside in search of Marvel's police detail. The officer was still in the parking lot.

"Have you seen Marvel?" RaShawn asked the officer as he approached the car.

"Not yet. He's still inside." The officer pointed to the car parked in front of his. "His car hasn't moved."

Britney pointed towards a Rolls Royce in the reserved parking space. "There's my mother's car. So she hasn't left yet either."

Marcus asked the officer to come with them as they rushed back into the church. Daniel Marson was behind the podium beginning his message, so most of the people had reclaimed their seats. RaShawn had instructed Rita to have a seat with the baby. He didn't know what they were about to encounter, but knew that Tyler needed to be as far from the scene as possible.

The rest of the gang ran from room to room asking anyone they encountered if they had seen either Marvel or Judge Hartman.

RaShawn's secretary told him, "I just opened your office. She wanted to speak with Pastor Williams in private. I hope that was okay."

"Thank you," he said as he rushed past her. As they reached the door, the police officer held them back.

"Knock on the door," the officer said.

RaShawn did as he was commanded.

"Yes?" a woman's voice from inside the room called out as if she were in her own office and had already asked not to be disturbed.

The police officer nodded at RaShawn, he then asked, "Is that you, Judge Hartman?"

"Bishop, why don't you come in and join us?" Judge Hartman asked.

RaShawn turned to the officer, he gave the okay and then RaShawn slowly opened the door to his office. He was caught off guard as he stood in the middle of his office staring at the gun in Judge Hartman's hand and the glass of wine in Williams' hand. "Don't drink it, Marvel. It's poison."

"What is wrong with you, Bishop Thomas? I thought you wanted him to repent and be cleansed from his sins?"

"Not like this," RaShawn told her.

The officer pointed his gun at Judge Hartman. "I'm only going to say this once, ma'am. Put the gun down and then stand up."

"Who do you think you are... barging in where you have no jurisdiction? I will have your badge, officer." Even while being caught red handed, Judge Hartman was cocky and unyielding.

"Give it up, Mother. It's over and you're going to jail," Britney told her.

Still holding the gun, Judge Hartman shook her head with disdain. "Everything I've done has been for you. But you have always been so ungrateful and hateful where I'm concerned. What more do you want from me, Britney?"

"You didn't do anything for me. Everything... all of it has been about you and your career. You never should have had a kid in the first place."

"That's what I tried to tell your father. But he promised to marry me if I had you. But we both know what a liar he turned out to be."

While Britney and Judge Hartman were arguing back and forth and the police officer stood there looking as if he didn't know what to do next, the window in RaShawn's office was quietly being raised. RaShawn glanced over and saw Detective Harris sliding through the window.

Judge Hartman was so angry with Britney that she stood up, waving the gun around. "You ungrateful little—"

"Put the gun down, Judge Hartman," the police officer demanded, getting into a shooting stance.

Judge Hartman was in no mood to listen. She turned to Marvel Williams and lifted the gun. Just before she pulled the trigger, Detective Harris lunged and knocked her to the ground. She was handcuffed and escorted out of the office.

Britney followed behind the officers. RaShawn told Marcus and his sister that he would catch up with them in the sanctuary and then turned back to Marvel, who appeared to be in shock. "You can put the drink down now, Marvel."

But Marvel didn't release the glass. Instead he stared at it as if it were the answer to all his problems. "I could drink this and be just fine with the outcome."

What do I do now, Lord? I didn't see this coming, RaShawn silently prayed as he dropped down to the seat next to Marvel.

Listen to him.

"You don't want to do this, Marvel. What you really need is someone to talk to… someone who will really listen. I'm ready to do that, if you'll give me a chance."

"All you want to do is judge me. You don't want to listen to me. I'm tired of people telling me how I let God down… nobody seems to care that God let me down."

"I care," RaShawn said in a low, calm voice. "How did it happen?"

Swirling the wine around in the glass, thoughts of bringing the glass to his lips and swallowing danced around his head. But before he did, Marvel decided to unburden himself. He turned to RaShawn and said, "What do you think of a man who takes care of God's house while his own falls apart?"

"I know it happens a lot."

"Some things should never happen." Tears rolled down Marvel's face as he admitted, "I thought having my wife with me while I traveled would keep women away from me. I never wanted to be the kind of preacher who cheats on his wife. But do you know what was happening to my son while we were out preaching from town to town for the Lord?"

This is going to be bad, isn't it Lord? RaShawn tried to keep the communication lines between him and God open, because he needed God's help.

It's going to be bad. My son is hurting.

"My father-in-law was molesting my son," Marvel choked out the words through his tears. "The Christian community judges me for marrying my son to another man. But what else was I supposed to do? I left him with that monster. I am responsible for what he's become, so I wasn't just going to turn my back on him again."

RaShawn was crying right along with Marvel. He leaned closer to the man he had so harshly judged and said, "I get it now, Marvel. You've carried the guilt of this in your heart for too long."

"I wouldn't have left him there, if I had known."

"I believe that. I'm sure your son knows that as well."

Anger boiled in Marvel and he barked, "God was supposed to protect my son."

"Your son was greatly wounded. I don't discount that. But you can't discount what God can do to heal him either."

"I prayed so many times for God to change his heart and mind about being gay, but it never happened."

"You know as well as I do that you can't just stop praying. What was done to your son was wrong. He was condemned to a life he probably wouldn't have chosen. But your not speaking out and telling him the truth with love, will condemn him to a hell that he won't be able to get out of. So, which is worse?"

"I don't know," Marvel cried out.

"I know," RaShawn told him. "The worst would be for you to die right now, and never have the chance to reconcile your relationship with God or to fight for your son's eternal soul. Then you really would have abandoned him."

116

Marvel looked at the glass of wine once more. Suddenly it didn't seem like the answer to all his problems. He put the drink down. Sat there for a minute trying to compose himself. Then he stood up. "I don't know if you're right or not, but if I die today, I'll never know. I'm going to go apologize to my son, and then I need to do what Marson did and talk to God... find out what path I'm supposed to take."

RaShawn picked up the glass and poured the contents out the window.

Chapter Fifteen

"You did good," Britney told him as she came into his office and Marvel walked out. She had just watched the police drive off with her mother. The whole ordeal made her want to just break down and cry. But she'd already shed too many tears over her mother's actions.

"How much did you hear?"

"Enough to understand his pain. I'll be praying for him and his son." Britney leaned against the cabinet as her head began to swim. She was seeing double and needed to steady herself.

"I wish I had known what he was dealing with. I'd like to think that I would've had a little more compassion."

Her head was pounding now, but she tried not to show it. "Like you just told Marvel, don't let the guilt eat you alive. The way I see it, we can't do anything about the past. But we can all move forward and let the Lord heal and cleanse us."

He walked over to her. "Thank you for being here with me." Leaning into her, RaShawn gently kissed her lips.

They then held on to each other like nothing else mattered but that moment.

But when he released her, she stumbled backward, and then grabbed hold of RaShawn's shirt, trying to steady herself.

"I figured I was a good kisser, but I had no idea that I could actually make someone swoon," he said jokingly.

"I-I think I need a doc—" she dropped to the floor before she could finish her statement.

As RaShawn watched Britney drop to the floor, it was as if his heart went with her. She couldn't be dead. Judge Hartman was on her way to jail, no way was he going to allow her to add one more victim to her list. He knelt down and felt for a pulse all the while praying for God to step in.

The pulse was there… it was faint, but still a living-you've-still-got-a-fighting-chance kind of pulse. He scooped Britney off the floor, grabbed his keys and ran like the church was on fire. He didn't know what could have caused Britney to suddenly faint like that, but he knew one thing for sure. He wasn't about to stand by and let her die… not like the others. He was here and he was going to do something.

"Where are you going? Marson is wrapping up. We need you in there to close us out for the day." His secretary practically chased him as he ran out of the church.

He placed Britney on the passenger's seat then ran to the driver's side while telling his secretary, "I've got to get her to the hospital. Tell Senior Bishop Brown to close us out." RaShawn jumped in the car and went from zero to sixty in a matter of seconds. He had no time to spare… had to get Britney to the hospital.

Britney's eyes fluttered as she grabbed hold of her head. "W-what happened?"

"It's my mom. She drug me. But I thought it was wearing off." Britney yawned and closed her eyes again.

He shook her. "Stay with me, Britney. Don't go back to sleep. Okay?"

"I'm tired," she said as she nodded back off.

Holding on to the wheel with one hand and shaking Britney with the other, he tried his best to wake her up, but she wasn't coming back to him this time.

"Sweet, sweet Jesus, don't let me down. Don't let her die on me." And in the instant he not only had compassion for Marvel Williams, but he understood how the man could have gone so far away from the will of God. If God didn't help Britney after all the years he'd spent on the mission field and behind a pulpit in service to Him, then RaShawn didn't know what that meant for the future.

He pulled into the emergency area of the hospital, jumped out of the car, carried Britney in his arms into the hospital hollering, "Help, I need help!"

A nurse had a bed brought out and Britney was wheeled through the double doors. RaShawn tried to follow, but the nurse asked him to stay behind and fill out the hospital forms. "Okay, but you need to know that she was drugged. I don't know what was used but she's not doing good."

"Thanks for telling me," the nurse said. "We'll take it from here."

RaShawn didn't want to leave Britney in their hands. He wanted to demand that he be allowed to follow, but he also didn't want to get in the way. So, he filled out the paperwork with as much information as he knew, then paced the floor waiting for the doctors to tell him something.

God had to come through for Britney. RaShawn and Britney had grown close over the last two years and he cared very deeply for her. The last time he lost someone he cared so deeply about was when he had been ten and his mom died. That loss had brought him closer to God. But could his faith handle another blow like that?

Realizing that he was on shaky ground, RaShawn gave the emergency room attendant his cell phone number and told her he would be in the chapel. Once he arrived at the chapel, RaShawn prostrated himself before the altar. Through tears and sweat, he prayed for Britney, begging the Lord to hear his plea and spare her life.

After he finished praying for Britney, he sat on one of the pew seats and prayed for himself. Because if things didn't turn out the way he wanted them to, RaShawn didn't want to stray away from His Lord and Savior. He didn't want anything to come between the relationship he'd built with his heavenly Father. Too many of his fellow preachers had allowed personal tragedies to steer them away from God and away from their mission. RaShawn refused to give up his mission, there were too many lives at stake. So, even though he very clearly knew what outcome he wanted for this situation, he found himself saying, "Your will be done, My Lord. Whatever it is, I will accept it."

He'd done all he could do, so he headed back to check on Britney. RaShawn was drained as he re-entered the emergency room. He barely had strength to make it to the check-in desk to ask about Britney. But just as the woman behind the check-in desk was telling him that there was no change in Britney's condition, someone touched his arm.

Turning around, RaShawn was blessed to see Mama-Carmella and his Dad. "Marcus is parking the car. We came as soon as your secretary told us what had happened."

RaShawn had never been so glad to see anyone. He hugged Mama-Carmella. And then went to his dad. The two men hugged. RaShawn tried to stay strong, but as his father wrapped his arms around him and said, "It's going to be alright, son," RaShawn could do nothing to stop the tears that fell like a waterfall. "What am I going to do if something happens to her, Dad?"

"Britney is going to be fine," Ramsey told him. "You've got to believe that."

Overwhelmed, RaShawn sat down and put his hands to his face. He held them there until he calmed down and then wiped the tears from his face. Carmella sat down next to him and put her hand on his arm. "You do believe, don't you?"

After talking with Marvel and realizing that sometimes God doesn't solve our problems, RaShawn had feared that this might be one of those times. But he hadn't been raised to doubt God. No matter how difficult the situation was, RaShawn had to believe in the God he served. He nodded. "I believe. Britney will survive."

As if God had been waiting for RaShawn to make his declaration, the double doors opened and the doctor walked over to him. "Are you RaShawn?"

Standing up, RaShawn said, "Yes. Is Britney okay?"

The doctor smiled. "She's asking for you. But she's a little sore right now because we had to pump her stomach. She's going to be our guest for a few days."

***

Once Britney had been assigned a room, his family left the hospital so he could spend time with her without being overwhelmed by having too many people in her room. He sat with her for hours. He was willing to talk about anything Britney wanted. And he never once brought up her mother, because he didn't want to upset her.

But Britney needed to talk about it, so after about an hour she said, "I still can't believe my mother is as evil as she is."

"I never would have guessed that she was the Avenger of Sins, not in a million years. After all, she was ticked at me for firing your uncle."

"He's not my uncle."

"What do you mean?" RaShawn's eyebrows went up. "Every time I talked to Tony Hartman, all he did was brag about his beautiful niece."

Pain etched across Britney's face as she told him, "Tony was my father. My mother killed him because he was finally going to tell me the truth and come clean to everyone. But in true fashion, Judge Lisa Hartman wasn't about to let a scandal cost her the career she had built."

To say that he was shocked would have been a great understatement. But he kept himself from gawking as he said, "If that's the reason she killed Tony, then why the whole Avenger of Sins charade, and why kill the other men?"

"My mother is a very complicated woman who has been hurt by men who claimed to be servants of God.

When I saw that 'you do right and I won't do wrong' phrase at Linden's house it shook me because I knew I had heard it before... my stepfather used to say that to me and my mother when he wanted us to do something that he knew we didn't want to do. I must have repressed that memory, but while my mother had me drugged out of my mind, it came back to me."

"I'm so sorry that you had to grow up with that man."

"You and me both," she responded. "My mother probably wouldn't have done the things she did, had she not been married to that monster." Shaking her head, Britney added, "I guess she figured she was doing the world a service by killing those other preachers along with Tony."

"So, do you think we were right about the reason Daniel Marson didn't get killed?" he asked.

"Since she's a judge it makes sense to me. She knew he wasn't guilty of anything, so even a person as crazy as she obviously couldn't go against her sense of justice."

It was crazy all right, that so many men had to die so that Judge Hartman could keep her secrets. He prayed that the woman spent a long time in prison and that she truly found Jesus while she was there... maybe he would go into prison ministry.

"I'm going to let you get some sleep, but I'll be back in the morning," RaShawn told her as he stood to leave.

The next morning RaShawn arrived at the hospital bright and early with a dozen roses. The morning after that he brought lilies. On the third morning, he brought orchids.

"You're spoiling me," Britney told him as she was preparing to be released. "When I get home I'm going to be looking for you to bring me flowers in the morning."

"I'll do it. What kind would you like tomorrow?" RaShawn asked, totally serious. Each day as he came to the hospital and sat with Britney and became mesmerized by her ability to weather the storm in her life, he realized that he didn't just care for her, he loved her and wanted nothing more than to be with her every day for the rest of his life.

She shook her head. "No more flowers, please. But you know, we never did go to dinner."

"I like the sound of dinner," RaShawn told her, "But I think I need a longer commitment from you than that."

"Oh my God, he's about to pop the question," came the voice of Mama-Carmella from behind him.

RaShawn and Britney turned toward the open door and were greeted by the gawking eyes of his family, plus Rita and Tyler. "How long have you all been standing there?"

"We knew Britney was being released from the hospital today. So, we wanted to come and see her before she left," Ramsey said.

"And I came to take her home," Rita said.

Then Raven said, "That's right, little bro, Britney is about to leave town, so I suggest you get on with this. The Marshall-Thomas family needs another wedding in our lives."

"You heard her," RaShawn said as he pulled Britney into his arms. "My family loves weddings. So, what do you say, huh? How about it?"

"Boy, if you don't stop being silly and get down on one knee," Mama-Carmella said.

But Britney stopped him from bending down. "You had me at 'huh,' and 'how about it' was just the icing on the cake. Of course I'll marry you... but I do have one condition."

"What's that?" RaShawn asked.

"That you don't fire any more preachers."

The End...

One

"I'm leaving you," Judge Nelson Marshall said, as he walked into the kitchen and stood next to the stainless steel prep table.

Taking a sweet potato soufflé out of her brand new Viking, dual-baking oven, Carmella was bobbing her head to Yolanda Adams's, "I Got the Victory", so she didn't hear Nelson walk into the kitchen.

He turned the music down and said, "Did you hear me, Carmella? I'm leaving."

Carmella put the soufflé on her prep table and turned toward Nelson. He was frowning, and she'd never known him to frown when she baked his favorite soufflé. Then she saw the suitcase in his hand and understood. Nelson hated to travel. His idea of the perfect vacation was staying home and renting movies for an entire week, but recently he had been attending one convention after another. And last week, he'd been in Chicago with her as she had to attend her brother's funeral.

Carmella was thankful that Nelson had taken vacation to attend the funeral with her, because she really didn't think she would have made it through that week without him. She and her younger brother had always been close, but after losing both their parents by the time they were in their thirties, the bond between them had become even stronger. Now she was trying to make sense of a world where forty-six-year-old men died of heart attacks.

Nelson had been fidgety the entire time they were in Chicago. She knew he hated being away from home, so she cut their trip short by a day. He hadn't told her he had another trip planned. "Not another one of those boring political conventions?"

He shook his head.

Nelson had almost lost his last bid for criminal court judge. Since then he had been obsessed with networking with government officials in hopes of getting appointed to a federal bench and bypassing elections altogether.

"Sit down, Carmella, we need to talk."

Carmella sat down on one of the stools in front of the kitchen island.

Nelson sat down next to Carmella. He lowered his head.

"Nelson, what's wrong?"

He didn't respond. But he had the same look on his face that he'd had the night they'd received the call about his grandmother's death.

"Please say something, honey. You're scaring me," Carmella said.

He lifted his head and attempted to look into his wife's eyes, but quickly turned away as he said, "This doesn't work for me anymore."

Confused, Carmella asked, "What's not working?"

"This marriage, Carmella. It's not what I want anymore."

"I don't understand, Nelson." She turned away from him and looked around her expansive kitchen. It had been redesigned a couple of years ago to ensure that she had everything she needed to throw the most lavish dinner parties that Raleigh, NC had ever seen. Nelson had told her that if he were ever going to get an appointment to a federal bench, he would need to network and throw fundraising campaigns for the senators and congressmen of North Carolina.

So she'd exchanged her kitchen table for a prep table, and installed the walk-in cooler to keep her salads and desserts at just the right temperature for serving. The Viking stove with its six burners and dual oven—one side convection and the other with an infrared broiler—had been her most expensive purchase. But the oven had been worth it. The infrared broiler helped her food to taste like restaurant-quality broiled food, and the convection side of the oven did amazing things with her pastries. She'd turned her home into a showplace in order to impress the guests who attended their legendary dinner parties. She had done everything Nelson had asked her to do, so Carmella couldn't understand why she was now in her kitchen listening to her husband say that he didn't want this anymore. "We've been happy, right?"

Nelson shook his head. "I haven't been happy with our marriage for a long time now."

"Then why didn't you say something? We could have gone to counseling or talked with Pastor Mitchell."

Nelson stood up. "It's too late for that. I've already filed for a divorce. All you need to do is sign the papers when you receive them, and then we can both move on with our lives."

Tears welled in Carmella's eyes as she realized that while she had been living in this house and sleeping in the same bed with Nelson, he had been seeing a divorce lawyer behind her back. "What about the kids, Nelson? What am I supposed to tell them?"

"Our children are grown, Carmella. You can't hide behind them anymore."

"What's that supposed to mean?" Carmella stood up, anger flashing in her eyes. "Dontae is only seventeen years old. He's still in high school and needs both his parents to help him make his transition into adulthood."

"I'm not leaving Dontae. He can come live with me if he wants."

"Oh, so now you want to take my son away from me, too? What's gotten into you, Nelson? When did you become so cruel?"

"I'm not trying to take Dontae away from you. I just know that raising a son can be difficult for a woman to do alone. So, I'm offering to take him with me."

"That's generous of you," Carmella said snidely. Then a thought struck her, and she asked, "Are you seeing someone? Is that it? Is this some midlife crisis that you're going through?"

"This is not about anyone else, Carmella. It's about the fact that we just don't work anymore."

Tears were flowing down her honey-colored cheeks. "But I still love you. I don't want a divorce."

"I don't have time to argue with you. Just sign the papers and let's get this over with."

She put her hands on her small hips and did the sista-sista neck roll, as her bob-styled hair swished from one side to the other. "We haven't argued in years. I have just gone with the flow and done whatever you wanted me to do. But on the day my husband packs his bags and asks me for a divorce, I think we should at least argue about that, don't you?"

He pointed at her and sneered as if her very presence offended him. "See, this is exactly why I waited so long to tell you. I knew you were going to act irrational."

"Irrational! Are you kidding me?" Carmella wanted to pull her hair out. The man standing in front of her was not her husband. He must have fallen, bumped his head and lost his fool mind. "What are we going to tell Joy and Dontae? I mean…you're not giving me anything to go on. We've been married twenty-five years and all of a sudden you just want out?"

"Like I said before, Joy and Dontae will be fine." He picked up his suitcase again and said, "I'm done discussing this. I'll be back to get the rest of my clothes. You should receive the divorce papers in a day or two. Just sign them and put them on the kitchen table." He headed toward the front door.

Following behind him, Carmella began screaming, "I'm not signing any divorce papers, so don't waste your time sending them here. And when you get off of whatever drug you're on, you'll be grateful that I didn't sign."

After opening the front door, Nelson turned to face his wife. With anger in his eyes, he said, "You better sign those papers or you'll regret it." He then stepped out of the house and slammed the door.

Carmella opened the door and ran after her husband. "Why are you doing this, Nelson? How am I supposed to pay the house note or our other bills if you leave me like this?"

"Get back in the house. You're making a scene."

"You spring this divorce on me without a second thought about my feelings, but you have the nerve to worry about the neighbors overhearing us?" Carmella shook her head in disgust. "I knew you were selfish, Nelson. But I never thought you were heartless."

He opened his car door and got in. "You're not going to make me feel guilty about this, Carmella. It's over between us. I want a divorce."

As Nelson backed out of the driveway, Carmella put her hands on her hips and shouted, "Well, you're not getting one!"

She stood barefoot, hands on hips, as Nelson turned what had seemed like an ordinary day into something awful and hideous. He backed out of the driveway—and out of her life— if what he said was to be believed. Carmella had been caught off guard...taken by surprise by this whole thing. Nelson had always been a family-values, family-first kind of man. He loved his children, and she'd thought he loved her as well. The family had attended church together and loved the Lord. But in the last year, Nelson had found one reason after another for not attending Sunday services.

"Are you okay?"

Carmella had been in a daze, watching Nelson drive out of her life; so she hadn't noticed that Cynthia Drake, their elderly next-door neighbor was outside doing her weekly gardening. Carmella wiped the tears from her face and turned toward the older woman.

"Is there anything I can do?" Cynthia asked, as she took off her gardening gloves.

"W-what just happened?" Carmella asked with confusion in her eyes.

"Come on," Cynthia said. She grabbed hold of Carmella's arm. "Let me get you back in the house."

"Why is everybody so obsessed with this house? It's empty, nobody in it but me. What am I supposed to do here alone?"

Cynthia guided Carmella back into the house and sat her down on the couch. "I'm going to get you something to drink." She disappeared into the kitchen and came back with a glass of iced tea and a can of Sunkist orange soda. "I didn't know which one you might want."

Carmella reached for the soda. "The iced tea is Nelson's. I don't drink it."

Cynthia sat down next to Carmella. She put her hand on Carmella's shoulder. "Do you want to talk?"

"Talk about what?" Carmella opened the Sunkist and took a sip. "I don't even know what's going on. I mean... I thought we were happy. I had no idea that Nelson wanted a divorce, but evidently, he's been planning this for a while."

"You need to get a divorce lawyer," Cynthia said.

"I don't want a divorce. I don't know what has gotten into Nelson, but he'll be back."

"You and Nelson have been married a long time, so I hope you're right. It would be a shame for him to throw away his marriage after all these years."

Carmella put the Sunkist down, put her head in her hands and started crying. This was too much for her. Nelson was the father of her children. He was supposed to love her for the rest of her life. They had stood before God and vowed to be there for each other, through the good and the bad, until death. How could he do this to her?

"Here, hon. Dry your face." Cynthia handed Carmella some tissue. "Do you have any family members that I could call to have them come sit with you for a while?"

"My parents have been dead for years and my only brother died last week," she said miserably.

"Oh hon, I'm so sorry to hear that."

Carmella lifted her hands and then let them flap back into her lap. "I just don't understand. I thought we were happy."

Sitting down next to Carmella, Cynthia said, "I've been married three times, and honey, trust me when I tell you that you'll probably never understand. Men don't need a reason for the things they do."

They sat talking for a while, and Carmella was comforted by the wise old woman who had taken time out from her gardening to sit with her in her time of need. When Cynthia was ready to leave, Carmella felt as if she should do something for the kindly old woman. She ran to the kitchen and came back with the sweet potato soufflé that she had lovingly fixed for her husband. She handed it to Cynthia, and said, "Thank you. I don't know what I would have done if you hadn't helped me back into the house."

"Oh, sweetie, it was no problem. You don't have to give me anything."

"I want to. I made this sweet potato soufflé for my husband. But since he doesn't want it, it would bring me great joy knowing that another family enjoyed it."

"Well, then I'll take it."

After Carmella walked Cynthia out, she went to the upstairs bathroom. She lit her bathroom candles, turned on the hot water and then poured some peach scented bubble bath in the water. She got into the tub, hoping to soak her weary bones until the ache in her heart drifted away. The warm water normally soothed her and took her mind off the things that didn't get done that day or the things that didn't turn out just the way she'd planned. Carmella enjoyed the swept-away feeling she experienced when surrounded by bubbles and her vanilla-scented candles. But tonight, all she felt was dread. She wondered if anyone would care if she drifted off to sleep, slid down all the way into the water and drowned like Whitney Houston had done.

The thought was tempting, because Carmella didn't know if she wanted to live without her husband. Tears rolled down her face as she realized that as much as she didn't want to live without Nelson, he was already living without her.

You've been reading an excerpt of…

Tears Fall at Night (Book 1)
Praise Him Anyhow Series

About the Author

Vanessa Miller is a best-selling author, playwright, and motivational speaker. She started writing as a child, spending countless hours either reading or writing poetry, short stories, stage plays and novels. Vanessa's creative endeavors took on new meaning in 1994 when she became a Christian. Since then, her writing has been centered on themes of redemption, often focusing on characters facing multi-dimensional struggles.

Vanessa's novels have received rave reviews, with several appearing on *Essence Magazine's* Bestseller's List. Miller's work has receiving numerous awards, including "Best Christian Fiction Mahogany Award" and the "Red Rose Award for Excellence in Christian Fiction." Miller graduated from Capital University with a degree in Organizational Communication. She is an ordained minister in her church, explaining, "God has called me to minister to readers and to help them rediscover their place with the Lord."

Vanessa has recently completed the For Your Love series for Kimani Romance and How Sweet the Sound for Abingdon Press, first book in a historical set in the Gospel era which releases March 2014. Vanessa is currently working on an ebook series of novellas in the Praise Him Anyhow series. She is also working on the My Soul to Keep series for Whitaker House.

Vanessa Miller's website address is: www.vanessamiller.com But you can also stay in touch with Vanessa by joining her mailing list @ http://

vanessamiller.com/events/join-mailing-list/ Vanessa can also be reached at these other sites as well:

Join me on Facebook: https://www.facebook.com/groups/77899021863/

Join me on Twitter: https://www.twitter.com/vanessamiller01

CPSIA information can be obtained at www.ICGtesting.com
Printed in the USA
LVOW10s1610091215

466131LV00020B/817/P